SWAMI AND FRIENDS

R. K. NARAYAN

INDIAN THOUGHT PUBLICATIONS

INDIAN THOUGHT PUBLICATIONS

New No.38, Thanikachalam Road,
T. Nagar, Chennai - 600 017
www.malgudi.co.in

© Legal Heirs of R. K. NARAYAN
SWAMI AND FRIENDS
ISBN: 978-81-85986-00-5

First Published in 1935 by
Hamish Hamilton, London

First Indian Edition 1944
55th Reprint 2011

Printed in India at

Sudarsan Graphics Private Limited
27, Neelakanta Mehta Street,
T.Nagar, Chennai - 600 017

TO MY PARENTS

1

MONDAY MORNING

It was Monday morning. Swaminathan was reluctant to open his eyes. He considered Monday specially unpleasant in the calendar. After the delicious freedom of Saturday and Sunday, it was difficult to get into the Monday mood of work and discipline. He shuddered at the very thought of school: that dismal yellow building; the fire-eyed Vedanayagam, his class-teacher; and the headmaster with his thin long cane...

By eight he was at his desk in his 'room', which was only a corner in his father's dressing-room. He had a table on which all his things, his coat, cap, slate, ink-bottle, and books, were thrown in a confused heap. He sat on his stool and shut his eyes to recollect what work he had for the day: first of course there was arithmetic—those five puzzles in profit and loss; then there was English—he had to copy down a page from his Eighth Lesson, and write dictionary meanings of difficult words; and then there was geography.

And only two hours before him to do all this heap of work and get ready for the school!

***

Fire-eyed Vedanayagam was presiding over the class with his back to the long window. Through its bars one saw a bit of the drill ground and a corner of the veranda of the Infant Standards. There were huge windows on the left showing vast open grounds bound at the other extreme by the railway embankment.

To Swaminathan existence in the classroom was possible only because he could watch the toddlers of the Infant Standards falling over one another, and through the windows on the left see the 12.30 mail gliding over the embankment, booming and rattling while passing over the Sarayu Bridge.

The first hour passed off quietly. The second they had arithmetic. Vedanayagam went out and returned in a few minutes in the role of an arithmetic teacher. He droned on monotonously. Swaminathan was terribly bored. His teacher's voice was beginning to get on his nerves. He felt sleepy.

The teacher called for home exercises. Swaminathan left his seat, jumped on the platform, and placed his notebook on the table. While the teacher was scrutinizing the sums, Swaminathan was gazing on his face, which seemed so tame at close quarters. His criticism of the teacher's face was that his eyes were too near each other, that there was more hair on his chin than one saw from the bench, and that he was very very bad-looking.

His reverie was disturbed. He felt a terrible pain in the soft flesh above his left elbow. The teacher was pinching him with one hand, and with the other crossing out all the sums. He wrote 'Very Bad' at the bottom of the page, flung the notebook in Swaminathan's face, and drove him back to his seat.

Next period they had history. The boys looked forward to it eagerly. It was taken by D. Pillai, who had earned a name in the school for kindness and good humour. He was reputed to have never frowned or sworn at the boys at any time. His method of teaching history conformed to no canon of education. He told the boys with a wealth of detail the private histories of Vasco da Gama, Clive, Hastings, and others. When he described the various fights in history, one heard the clash of arms and the groans of the slain. He was the despair of the headmaster whenever the latter stole along the corridor with noiseless steps on his rounds of inspection.

The scripture period was the last in the morning. It was not such a dull hour after all. There were moments in it that brought stirring pictures before one: the Red Sea cleaving and making way for the Israelites; the physical feats of Samson; Jesus rising from the grave; and so on. The only trouble was that the scripture master, Mr. Ebenezar, was a fanatic.

"Oh, wretched idiots!" the teacher said, clenching his fists. "Why do you worship dirty, lifeless, wooden idols and stone images? Can they talk? No. Can they see? No. Can they bless you? No. Can they take you to heaven? No. Why? Because they have no life. What did your gods do when Muhammad of Gazni smashed them to pieces, trod upon them, and constructed out of them steps for his lavatory? If those idols and images had life, why did they not parry Muhammad's onslaughts?"

He then turned to Christianity. "Now see our Lord Jesus. He could cure the sick, relieve the poor, and take us to heaven. He was a real God. Trust him and he will take you to heaven; the kingdom of heaven is within us." Tears rolled down Ebenezar's cheeks when he pictured Jesus before him. Next moment his face became purple with rage as he thought of Sri Krishna: "Did our Jesus go gadding about with dancing girls like your Krishna? Did our Jesus go about stealing butter like that arch-scoundrel Krishna? Did our Jesus practise dark tricks on those around him?"

He paused for breath. The teacher was intolerable today. Swaminathan's blood boiled. He got up and asked, "If he did not, why was he crucified?" The teacher told him that he might come to him at the end of the period and learn it in private. Emboldened by this mild reply, Swaminathan put to him another question, "If he was a god, why did he eat flesh and fish and drink wine?" As a *brahmin* boy it was inconceivable to him that a god should be a non-vegetarian. In answer to this, Ebenezar left his seat, advanced slowly towards Swaminathan, and tried to wrench his left ear off.

***

Next day Swaminathan was at school early. There was still half an hour before the bell. He usually spent such an interval in running round the school or in playing the Digging Game under the huge tamarind tree. But today he sat apart, sunk in thought. He had a thick letter in his pocket. He felt guilty when he touched its edge with his fingers.

He called himself an utter idiot for having told his father about Ebenezar the night before during the meal.

As soon as the bell rang, he walked into the headmaster's room and handed him a letter. The headmaster's face became serious when he read:

SIR,

I beg to inform you that my son Swaminathan of the First Form, A section, was assaulted by his scripture master yesterday in a fanatical rage. I hear that he is always most insulting and provoking in his references to the Hindu religion. It is bound to have a bad effect upon the boys. This is not the place for me to dwell upon the necessity for toleration in these matters.

I am also informed that when my son got up to have a few doubts cleared, he was roughly handled by the same teacher. His ears were still red when he came home last evening.

The one conclusion that I can come to is that you do not want non-Christian boys in your school. If it is so, you may kindly inform us as we are quite willing to withdraw our boys and send them elsewhere. I may remind you that Albert Mission School is not the only school that this town, Malgudi, possesses. I hope you will be kind enough to inquire into the matter and favour me with a reply. If not, I regret to inform you, I shall be constrained to draw the attention of higher authorities to these unchristian practices.

I have the honour to be,

Sir,

Your most obedient servant,

W. T. Srinivasan.

When Swaminathan came out of the room, the whole school crowded round him and hung on his lips. But he treated inquisitive questions with haughty indifference.

He honoured only four persons with his confidence. Those were the four that he liked and admired most in his class. The first was Somu, the monitor, who carried himself with such an easy air. He set about his business, whatever it was, with absolute confidence and calmness. He was known to be chummy even with the teachers. No teacher ever put to him a question in the class. It could not be said that he shone brilliantly as a student. It was believed that only the headmaster could reprimand him. He was more or less the uncle of the class.

Then there was Mani, the Mighty Good-For-Nothing. He towered above all the other boys of the class. He seldom brought any books to the class, and never bothered about homework. He came to the class, monopolized the last bench, and slept bravely. No teacher ever tried to prod him. It was said that a new teacher who once tried it very nearly lost his life. Mani bullied all strangers that came his way, be they big or small. People usually slunk aside when he passed. Wearing his cap at an angle, with a Tamil novel under his arm, he had been coming to the school ever since the old school peon could remember. In most of the classes he stayed longer than his friends did. Swaminathan was proud of his friendship. While others crouched in awe, he could address him as 'Mani' with gusto and pat him on the back familiarly. Swaminathan admiringly asked whence Mani derived his power. Mani replied that he had a pair of wooden clubs at home with which he would break the backs of those that dared to tamper with him.

Then there was Sankar, the most brilliant boy of the class. He solved any problem that was given to him in five minutes, and always managed to border on ninety per cent. There was a belief among a section of the boys that if only he started cross-examining the teachers, the teachers would be nowhere. Another section asserted that Sankar was a dud and that he learnt all the problems and their solution in advance by his sycophancy. He was said to receive his ninety per cent as a result of washing clothes for his masters. He could speak to the teachers in English in the open class. He knew all the rivers, mountains, and countries in the world. He could repeat history in his sleep. Grammar was child's play to him. His face was radiant with intelligence, though his nose was almost always damp, and though he came to the class with his hair braided and with flowers in it, Swaminathan looked on him as a marvel. He was very happy when he made Mani see eye to eye with him and admit Sankar to their company. Mani liked him in his own way and brought down his heavy fist on Sankar's back whenever he felt inclined to demonstrate his affection. He would scratch his head and ask where the blithering fool of a scraggy youngster got all that brain from and why he should not part with a little of it.

The fourth friend was Samuel, known as 'the Pea' on account of his size. There was nothing outstanding about him. He was just ordinary, no outstanding virtue of muscle or intellect. He was as bad in arithmetic as Swaminathan was. He was as apprehensive, weak, and nervous about things as Swaminathan was. The bond between them was laughter. They were able to see together the same absurdities and incongruities in things. The most trivial and unnoticeable thing to others would tickle them to death.

When Swaminathan told them what action his father had taken in the scripture master affair, there was a murmur of approval. Somu was the first to express it, by bestowing on his admirer a broad grin. Sankar looked serious and said, "Whatever others might say, you did right in setting your father to the job." The mighty Mani half closed his eyes and grunted an approval of sorts. He was only sorry that the matter should have been handled by elders. He saw no sense in it. Things of this kind should not be allowed to go beyond the four walls of the classroom. If he were Swaminathan, he would have closed the whole incident at the beginning by hurling an ink-bottle, if nothing bigger was available, at the teacher. Well, there was no harm in what Swaminathan had done; he would have done infinitely worse by keeping quiet. However, let the scripture master look out: Mani had decided to wring his neck and break his back.

Samuel the Pea found himself in an acutely embarrassing position. On the one hand, he felt constrained to utter some remark. On the other, he was a Christian and saw nothing wrong in Ebenezar's observations, which seemed to be only an amplification of one of the Commandments. He felt that his right place was on Ebenezar's side. He managed to escape by making scathing comments on Ebenezar's dress and appearance and leaving it at that.

The class had got wind of the affair. When the scripture period arrived there was a general expectation of some dramatic *dénouement*. But nothing happened. Ebenezar went on as merrily as ever. He had taken the trouble that day to plod through *Bhagavadgita*, and this generous piece of writing lends itself to any interpretation. In Ebenezar's hand it served as a weapon against Hinduism.

His tone was as vigorous as ever, but in his denunciation there was more scholarship. He pulled *Bhagavadgita* to pieces, after raising Hinduism on its base. Step by step he was reaching the sublime heights of rhetoric. The class Bible lay uncared for on the table.

The headmaster glided in.

Ebenezar halted, pushing back his chair, and rose, greatly flurried. He looked questioningly at the headmaster. The headmaster grimly asked him to go on. Ebenezar had meanwhile stealthily inserted a finger into the pages of the closed Bible. On the word of command from the headmaster, he tried to look sweet and relaxed his brow, which was knit in fury. He then opened his book where the finger marked and began to read at random. It happened to be the Nativity of Christ. The great event had occurred. There the divine occupant was in the manger. The Wise Men of the East were faithfully following the Star.

The boys attended in their usual abstracted way. It made little difference to them whether Ebenezar was making a study of Hinduism in the light of *Bhagavadgita* or was merely describing the Nativity of Christ.

The headmaster listened for a while and, in an undertone, demanded an explanation. They were nearing the terminal examination and Ebenezar had still not gone beyond the Nativity. When would he reach the Crucifixion and Resurrection, and begin to revise? Ebenezar was flabbergasted. He could not think of anything to say. He made a bare escape by hinting that that particular day of the week he usually devoted to a rambling revision. Oh, no! He was not as far behind as that. He was in the proximity of the Last Supper.

At the end of the day Swaminathan was summoned to the headmaster's room. As soon as he received the note, he had an impulse to run home. And when he expressed it, Mani took him in his hands, propelled him through to the headmaster's room, and gave him a gentle push in. Swaminathan staggered before the headmaster.

Ebenezar was sitting on a stool, looking sheepish. The headmaster asked: "What is the trouble, Swaminathan?"

"Oh—nothing, sir," Swaminathan replied.

"If it is nothing, why this letter?"

"Oh!" Swaminathan ejaculated uncertainly.

Ebenezar attempted to smile. Swaminathan wished to be well out of the whole affair. He felt he would not mind if a hundred Ebenezars said a thousand times worse things about the gods.

"You know why I am here?" asked the headmaster.

Swaminathan searched for an answer: the headmaster might be there to receive letters from boys' parents; he might be there to flay Ebenezars alive; he might be there to deliver six cuts with his cane every Monday at twelve o'clock. And above all why this question?

"I don"t know, sir," Swaminathan replied innocently.

"I am here to look after you," said the headmaster.

Swaminathan was relieved to find that the question had such a simple answer.

"And so," continued the headmaster, "you must come to me if you want any help, before you go to your father." Swaminathan furtively glanced at Ebenezar, who writhed in his chair.

"I am sorry," said the headmaster, "that you should have been so foolish as to go to your father about this simple matter. I shall look into it. Take this letter to your father."

Swaminathan took the letter and shot out of the room with great relief.

2

RAJAM AND MANI ·

River Sarayu was the pride of Malgudi. It was some ten minutes' walk from Ellaman Street, the last street of the town, chiefly occupied by oilmongers. Its sandbanks were the evening resort of all the people of the town. The Municipal President took any distinguished visitor to the top of the town hall and proudly pointed to him Sarayu in moonlight, glistening like a silver belt across the north.

The usual evening crowd was on the sand. Swaminathan and Mani sat aloof on a river-step, with their legs dangling in water. The *peepul* branches overhanging the river rustled pleasantly. A light breeze played about the boughs and scattered stray leaves on the gliding stream below. Birds filled the air with their cries. Far away, near Nallappa's Mango Grove, a little downstream, a herd of cattle was crossing the river. And then a country cart drawn by bullocks passed, the cart-man humming a low tune. It was some fifteen minutes past sunset and there was a soft red in the west.

"The water runs very deep here, doesn't it?" Mani asked.

"Yes, why?"

"I am going to bring Rajam here, bundle him up, and throw him into the river."

Rajam was a fresh arrival in the First A. He had sauntered into the class on the reopening day of the second term, walked up to the last bench, sat beside Mani, and felt very comfortable indeed till Mani gave him a jab in the ribs, which he returned. He had impressed the whole class on the very first day. He was a newcomer; he dressed very well—he was the only boy in the class who wore socks and shoes, fur cap and tie, and a wonderful coat and knickers. He came to the school in a car. As well as all this, he proved to be a very good student too. There were vague rumours that he had come from some English boys' school somewhere in Madras. He spoke very good English, "exactly like a 'European'"; which meant that few in the school could make out what he said. Many of his class-mates could not trust themselves to speak to him, their fund of broken English being small. Only Sankar, the genius of the class, had the courage to face him, though his English sounded halting and weak before that of Rajam.

This Rajam was a rival to Mani. In his manner to Mani he assumed a certain nonchalance to which Mani was not accustomed. If Mani jabbed, Rajam jabbed; if Mani clouted, he clouted; if Mani kicked, he kicked. If Mani was the overlord of the class, Rajam seemed to be nothing less. And add to all this the fact that Rajam was a regular seventy-percenter, second only to Sankar. There were sure indications that Rajam was the new power in the class. Day by day as Mani looked on, it was becoming increasingly clear that a new menace had appeared in his life.

All this lay behind his decision on the river-step to bundle up Rajam and throw him into the river. Swaminathan expressed a slight fear: "You forget that his father is the Police Superintendent." Mani remained silent for a while and said, "What do I care? Some night I am going to crack his shoulders with my clubs." ↑

"If I were you, I would keep out of the way of policemen. They are an awful lot," said Swaminathan.

"If you were me! Huh! But thank God I am not you, a milk-toothed coward like you."

Swaminathan bit his lips and sighed.

"And that reminds me," said the other, "you are in need of a little warning. I find you hanging about that Rajam a bit too much. Well, have a care for your limbs. That is all I can say."

Swaminathan broke into loud protestations. Did Mani think that Swaminathan could respect anyone but him, Mani the dear old friend and guide? What made him think so? As far as Swaminathan could remember, he had never been within three yards of Rajam. Oh, how he hated him! That vile upstart! When had Mani seen him with Rajam? Oh, yes, it must have been during the drawing period on Monday. It was Rajam who had come and talked to him in spite of the cold face that Swaminathan had turned to him. That ass had wanted a pencil-sharpener, which he did not get, as he was promptly directed to go to a shop and buy it if he needed it so urgently. Oh, there was no comparison between Rajam and Mani.

This pleased Mani greatly. For the first time that evening he laughed, and laughed heartily too. He shook Swaminathan and gave such an affectionate twist to his ear that Swaminathan gave a long howl. And then he suddenly asked, "Did you bring the thing that I wanted?"

"Oh, Mani! I beg a hundred pardons of you. My mother was all the time in the kitchen. I could not get it." ('It' referred to lime pickles.)

"You are a nasty little coward—Oh, this river-bank and the fine evening. How splendid it would have been!"

***

Swaminathan was to act as a cord of communication between Rajam and Mani. They were sitting on the last bench with their backs against the yellow wall. Swaminathan sat between Rajam and Mani. Their books were before them on the desks; but their minds were busy.

Mani wrote on a piece of paper "Are you a man?" and gave it to Swaminathan, who pushed it across to Rajam, putting on as offensive a look as possible, Rajam read it, crumpled it, and threw it away. At which Mani wrote another note repeating the question, with the addition "You are the son of a dog if you don't answer this," and pushed it across. Rajam hissed into Swaminathan's face, "You scoundrel, don't disturb me," and crumpled the letter.

Further progress was stopped.

"Swaminathan, stand up," said the teacher. Swaminathan stood up faithfully.

"What is Lisbon famous for?" asked the teacher.

Swaminathan hesitated and ventured, "For being the capital of Spain."

The teacher bit his moustache and fired a second question, "What do you know about the Indian climate?"

"It is hot in summer and cold in winter."

"Stand up on the bench!" roared the teacher. And Swaminathan stood up without a protest. He was glad that he was given this supposedly degrading punishment instead of the cane.

The teacher resumed his lessons: Africa was a land of forests. Nile was the most important river there. Did they understand? What did he say? He selected someone from the first bench to answer this question. (Nile was the most important river in Africa, the boy answered promptly, and the teacher was satisfied.) What was Nile? (The most important river in Africa, a boy answered with alacrity and was instantly snubbed for it, for he had to learn not to answer before he was asked to.) Silence. Silence. Why was there such a lot of noise in the class? Let them go on making a noise and they would get a clean, big zero in the examination. He would see to that...

Swaminathan paid no attention to the rest of the lessons. His mind began to wander. Standing on the bench, he stood well over the whole class. He could see so many heads, and he classified them according to the caps: there were four red caps, twenty-five Gandhi caps, ten fur caps, and so on.

When the work for the day was over, Swaminathan, Mani, and Rajam adjourned to a secluded spot to say what was in their minds. Swaminathan stood between them and acted as the medium of communication. They were so close that they could have heard each other even if they had spoken in whispers. But it was a matter of form between enemies to communicate through a medium. Mani faced Swaminathan steadily and asked, "Are you a man?" Swaminathan turned to Rajam and repeated, "Are you a man?" Rajam flared up and shouted, "Which dog doubts it?" Swaminathan turned to Mani and said ferociously, "Which dirty dog doubts it?"

"Have you the courage to prove that you are a man?" asked Mani.

Swaminathan turned to Rajam and repeated it.

"How?"

"How?" repeated Swaminathan to Mani.

"Meet me at the river, near Nallappa's Grove, tomorrow evening."

"—Near Nallappa's Grove," Swaminathan was pleased to echo.

"What for?" asked Rajam.

"To see if you can break my head."

"Oh, to pieces," said Rajam.

Swaminathan's services were dispensed with. They gave him no time to repeat their words. Rajam shouted in one ear, and Mani in the other.

"So we may expect you at the river tomorrow," said Swaminathan.

"Yes," Rajam assured them.

Mani wanted to know if the other would come with guards. No, he would not. And Mani voiced another doubt: "If anything happens to you, will you promise to keep it out of your father's knowledge?" Rajam promised, after repudiating the very suggestion that he might act otherwise.

✳✳✳

Nallappa's Grove stood a few yards before them. It was past six and the traffic for the day between the banks was over. The usual evening crowd was far behind them. Swaminathan and Mani were squatting on the sand. They were silent. Mani was staring at the ground, with a small wooden club under his arm. He was thinking: he was going to break Rajam's head in a short while and throw his body into the river. But if it should be recovered? But then how could they know that he had done it? But if Rajam should come and

19

trouble him at night as a spirit? Since his grandfather's death, he was sleeping alone. What if Rajam should come and pull his hair at night? After all it would be better not to kill him. He would content himself with breaking his limbs and leaving him to his fate. If he should batter his head, who was going to find it out? Unless of course—He cast a sly look at Swaminathan, who was blinking innocently... Unless of course Swaminathan informed the police.

At the sound of the creaking of boots, they turned and found that Rajam had come. He was dressed in khaki, and carried under his arm an airgun that was given to him a couple of months ago on his birthday. He stood very stiff and said: "Here I am, ready."

"You are late."

"Yes."

"We will start."

Rajam shouldered his gun and fired a shot in the air. Mani was startled. He stood still, his club down.

"You heard the shot?" asked Rajam. "The next is going to be into your body, if you are keen upon a fight."

"But this is unfair. I have no gun while you have... It was to be a hand-to-hand fight."

"Then why have you brought your club? You never said anything about it yesterday."

Mani hung down his head.

"What have I done to offend you?" asked Rajam.

"You called me a sneak before someone."

"That is a lie."

There was an awkward pause. "If this is all the cause of your anger, forget it. I won't mind being friends."

"Nor I," said Mani.

Swaminathan gasped with astonishment. In spite of his posing before Mani he admired Rajam intensely, and longed to be his friend. Now this was the happiest conclusion to all the unwanted trouble. He danced with joy. Rajam lowered his gun, and Mani dropped his club. To show his goodwill, Rajam pulled out of his pocket half a dozen biscuits.

The river's mild rumble, the rustling of the *peepul* leaves, the half-light of the late evening, and the three friends eating, and glowing with new friendship— Swaminathan felt at perfect peace with the world.

3

SWAMI'S GRANDMOTHER

In the ill-ventilated dark passage between the front hall and the dining-room, Swaminathan's grandmother lived with all her belongings, which consisted of an elaborate bed made of five carpets, three bed sheets, and five pillows, a square box made of jute fibre, and a small wooden box containing copper coins, cardamoms, cloves, and areca nut.

After the night meal, with his head on his granny's lap, nestling close to her, Swaminathan felt very snug and safe in the faint atmosphere of cardamom and cloves.

"Oh, Granny!" he cried ecstatically. "You don't know what a great fellow Rajam is." He told her the story of the first enmity between Rajam and Mani and the subsequent friendship.

"You know, he has a real police dress," said Swaminathan.

"Is it? What does he want a police dress for?" asked Granny.

"His father is the Police Superintendent. He is the master of every policeman here." Granny was impressed. She said that it must be a tremendous office indeed. She then recounted the days when her husband, Swaminathan's grandfather, was a powerful submagistrate, in which office he made the police force tremble before him, and the fiercest dacoits of the place flee. Swaminathan waited impatiently for her to finish the story. But she went on, rambled, confused, mixed up various incidents that took place at different times.

"That will do, Granny," he said ungraciously. "Let me tell you something about Rajam. Do you know how many marks he gets in arithmetic?"

"He gets all the marks, does he, child?" asked Granny.

"No, silly. He gets ninety marks out of one hundred."

"Good. But you must also try and get marks like him…You know, Swami, your grandfather used to frighten the examiners with his answers sometimes. When he answered a question, he did it in a tenth of the time that others took to do it. And then, his answers would be so powerful that his teachers would give him two hundred marks sometimes…When he passed his F.A. he got such a big medal! I wore it as a pendant for years till—when did I remove it? Yes, when your aunt was born…No, it wasn't your aunt…It was when your father was born…I remember on the tenth day of confinement…No, no. I was right. It was when your aunt was born. Where is that medal now? I gave it away to your aunt—and she melted it and made four bangles out of it. The fool! And such flimsy bangles too! I have always maintained that she is the worst fool in our family…"

"Oh, enough, Granny! You go on bothering about old unnecessary stories. Won't you listen to Rajam?"

"Yes, dear, yes."

"Granny, when Rajam was a small boy, he killed a tiger."

"Indeed! The brave little boy!"

"You are saying it just to please me. You don't believe it."

Swaminathan started the story enthusiastically: Rajam's father was camping in a forest. He had his son with him. Two tigers came upon them suddenly, one knocking down the father from behind. The other began chasing Rajam, who took shelter behind a bush and shot it dead with his gun. "Granny, are you asleep?" Swaminathan asked at the end of the story.

"No, dear, I am listening."

"Let me see. How many tigers came upon how many?"

"About two tigers on Rajam," said Granny.

Swaminathan became indignant at his grandmother's inaccuracy. "Here I am going hoarse telling you important things and you fall asleep and imagine all sorts of nonsense. I am not going to tell you anything more. I know why you are so indifferent. You hate Rajam."

"No, no, he is a lovely little boy," Granny said with conviction, though she had never seen Rajam. Swaminathan was pleased. Next moment a new doubt assailed him. "Granny, probably you don't believe the tiger incident."

"Oh, I believe every word of it," Granny said soothingly. Swaminathan was pleased, but added as a warning: "He would shoot anyone that called him a liar."

Granny expressed her approval of this attitude and then begged leave to start the story of *Harichandra*, who, just to be true to his word, lost his throne, wife, and child, and got them all back in the end. She was halfway through it when Swaminathan's rhythmic snoring punctuated her narration, and she lay down to sleep.

***

Saturday afternoon. Since Saturday and Sunday came so rarely, to Swaminathan it seemed absurd to waste them at home, gossiping with Granny and Mother or doing sums. It was his father's definite orders that Swaminathan should not start loafing in the afternoon and that he should stay at home and do school work. But this order was seldom obeyed.

Swaminathan sat impatiently in his 'study', trying to wrest the meaning out of a poem in his *English*

Reader. His father stood before the mirror, winding a turban round his head. He had put on his silk coat. Now only his spectacles remained. Swaminathan watched his progress keenly. Even the spectacles were on. All that now remained was the watch.

Swaminathan felt glad. This was the last item and after that Father would leave for the court. Mother came in with a tumbler of water in one hand and a plate of betel leaves and nuts in the other. Father drank the water and held out his hand. She gave him a little areca nut and half a dozen neatly-rolled betel leaves. He put them all into his mouth, chewing them with great contentment. Swaminathan read at the top of his voice the poem about a woolly sheep. His father fussed about a little for his tiny silver snuff-box and the spotted kerchief, which was the most unwashed thing in that house. He hooked his umbrella on his arm. This was really the last signal for starting. Swaminathan had almost closed the book and risen. His father had almost gone out of the room. But—Swaminathan stamped his foot under the table. Mother stopped Father and said: "By the way, I want some change. The tailor is coming today. He has been pestering me for the last four days."

"Ask him to come tomorrow," Father said. Mother was insistent. Father returned to his bureau, searched for the keys, opened it, took out a purse, and gave her the change. "I don't know how I am going to manage things for the rest of the month," he said, peering into the purse. He locked the bureau, and adjusted his turban before the mirror. He took a heavy pinch of snuff and, wiping his nose with his kerchief, walked out. Swaminathan heaved a sigh of relief.

"Bolt the door," came Father's voice from the street door. Swaminathan heard the clicking of the bolts. He sat at the window, watched his father turn the corner, and then left his post.

His mother was in the kitchen giving instructions to the cook about the afternoon coffee. Granny was sitting up in her bed. "Come here, boy," she cried as soon as she saw him.

"I can't. No time now."

"Please. I will give you three paise," she cried.

Swaminathan ignored the offer and dashed away.

"Where are you going?" Mother asked.

"I have got to go," Swaminathan said with a serious face.

"Are you going to loaf about in the sun?"

"Certainly not," he replied curtly.

"Wander about recklessly and catch fever?..."

"No, Mother, I am not going to wander about."

"Has your father not asked you to stay at home on holidays?"

"Yes, but my drawing master has asked me to see him. I suppose even then I should not go." He added bitterly: "If I fail in the drawing examination I think you will be pleased."

***

Swaminathan ran down Grove Street, turned to his right, threaded his way through Abu Lane, stood before a low-roofed, dingy house, and gave a low whistle. He waited for a second and repeated it. The door-chain clanked, the door opened a little, and Mani's head appeared and said: "Fool! My aunt is here, don't come in. Go away and wait for me there."

Swaminathan moved away and waited under a tree. The sun was beating down fiercely. The street was almost deserted. A donkey was standing near a gutter, patiently watching its sharp shadow. A cow was munching a broad, green, plantain leaf. Presently Mani sneaked out of his house.

Rajam's father lived in Lawley Extension (named after the mighty engineer Sir Frederick Lawley, who was at one time the Superintending Engineer for Malgudi Circle), which consisted of about fifty neat bungalows, mostly occupied by government officials. The trunk road to Trichinopoly passed a few yards in front of these houses.

Swaminathan and Mani were nervously walking up the short drive leading to Rajam's house. A policeman in uniform cried to them to stop and came running towards them. Swaminathan felt like turning and fleeing. He appealed to Mani to speak to the policeman. The policeman asked what they were doing there. Mani said in a tone in which overdone carelessness was a trifle obvious: "If Rajam is in the house, we are here to see him. He asked us to come." The policeman at once became astonishingly amiable and took them along to Rajam's room.

To Mani and Swaminathan the room looked large. There were chairs in it, actually chairs, and a good big table with Rajam's books arranged neatly on it. What impressed them most was a timepiece on the table. Such a young fellow to own a timepiece! His father seemed to be an extraordinary man.

Presently Rajam entered. He had known that his friends were waiting for him, but he liked to keep them waiting for a few minutes, because he had seen his father doing it. So he stood for a few minutes in the adjoining room, biting his nails. When he could keep away no longer, he burst in upon his friends.

"Sit down, boys, sit down," he cried when he saw them standing.

In a few minutes they were chatting about odds and ends, discussing their teachers and schoolmates, their parents, toys, and games.

Rajam took them to a cupboard and threw it open. They beheld astounding things in it, miniature trains and motors, mechanical marvels, and a magic lantern with slides, a good many large picture-books, and a hundred other things. What interested Mani most was a grim airgun that stood in a corner. Rajam gave them permission to handle anything they pleased. In a short while Swaminathan was running an engine all over the room. Mani was shooting arrow after arrow from a bow, at the opposite wall. When he tired of it, he took up the gun and devastated the furniture around with lead balls.

"Are you fellows, any of you, hungry?" Rajam asked.

"No," they said half-heartedly.

"Hey," Rajam cried. A policeman entered.

"Go and ask the cook to bring some coffee and tiffin for three." The ease and authority with which he addressed the policeman filled his friends with wonder and admiration.

The cook entered with a big plateful of eatables. He set down the plate on the table. Rajam felt that he must display his authority.

"Remove it from the table, you—" he roared at the cook. The cook removed it and placed it on a chair.

"You dirty ass, take it away, don't put it there."

"Where am I to put it, Raju?" asked the cook.

Rajam burst out: "You rascal, you scoundrel, you talk back to me?"

The cook made a wry face and muttered something.

"Put it on the table," Rajam commanded. The cook obeyed, mumbling: "If you are rude, I am going to tell your mother."

"Go and tell her, I don't care," Rajam retorted.

He peered into a cup and cursed the cook for bringing it so dirty. The cook looked up for a moment, quietly lifted the plate, and saying, "Come and eat in the kitchen if you want food," went away with it.

This was a great disappointment to Swaminathan and Mani, who were waiting with watering mouths. To Rajam it was a terrible moment. To be outdone by his servant before his friends! He sat still for a few minutes and then said with a forced laugh: "The scoundrel, that cook is a buffoon... Wait a minute." He went out.

After a while he returned, carrying the plate himself. His friends were a bit astonished at this sign of defeat. Obviously he could not subdue the cook. Swaminathan puzzled his head to find out why Rajam did not shoot the cook dead, and Mani wanted to ask if he could be allowed to have his own way with the cook for a few minutes. But Rajam set their minds at rest by explaining to them: "I had to bring this myself. I went in and gave the cook such a kick for his impertinence that he is lying unconscious in the kitchen."

4

"WHAT IS A TAIL?"

The geography master was absent, and the boys of the First A had leisure between three and three forty-five on Wednesday.

Somehow Swaminathan had missed his friends and found himself alone. He wandered along the corridor of the Infant Standards. To Swaminathan, who did not really stand over four feet, the children of the Infant Standards seemed ridiculously tiny. He felt vastly superior and old. He was filled with contempt when he saw them dabbling in wet clay, trying to shape models. It seemed such a meaningless thing to do at school! Why, they could as well do those things resembling elephants, mangoes, and whatnots, in the backyards of their houses. Why did they come all the way to a school to do this sort of thing? Schools were meant for more serious things like geography, arithmetic, Bible, and English.

In one room he found all the children engaged in repeating simultaneously the first two letters of the Tamil alphabet. He covered his ears and wondered how the teacher was able to stand it. He passed on. In another room he found an ill-clad, noisy crowd of children. The noise that they made, sitting on their benches and swinging their legs, got on his nerves. He wrinkled his brow and twisted his mouth in the hope of making the teacher feel his resentment; but unfortunately the teacher was sitting with his back to Swaminathan.

He paused at the foot of the staircase leading to the senior classes—the second and the third forms. He wanted to go up and inspect those classes which he eagerly looked forward to joining. He took two or three steps up, and changed his mind. The headmaster might be up there, he always handled those classes. The teachers too were formidable, not to speak of the boys themselves, who were snobs and bullies. He heard the creak-creak of sandals far off and recognized the footsteps of the headmaster. He did not want to be caught there—that would mean a lot of unsatisfactory explanations.

It was with pleasant surprise that he stumbled into his own set, which he had thought was not at school. Except Rajam and Mani all the rest were there. Under the huge tamarind tree they were playing some game. Swaminathan joined them with a low, ecstatic cry. The response disappointed him. They turned their faces to him with a faint smile, and returned to their game. What surprised Swaminathan most was that even the genial Somu was grim. Something seemed to be wrong somewhere. Swaminathan assumed an easy tone and shouted: "Boys, what about a little place for me in the game?" Nobody answered this. Swaminathan paused and announced that he was waiting for a place in the game.

"It is a pity, we can't take more," Sankar said curtly.

"There are people who can be very efficient as tails," said the Pea. The rest laughed at this.

"You said tail, didn't you?" asked Sankar. "What makes you talk of tail now?"

"It is just my pleasure. What do you care? It doesn't apply to you anyway," said the Pea.

"I am glad to hear it, but does it apply to anyone here?" asked Sankar.

"It may."

"What is a tail?"

"A long thing that attaches itself to an ass or a dog."

Swaminathan could comprehend very little except that the remark contained some unpleasant references to himself. His cheeks grew hot. He wanted to cry.

The bell rang and they ran to their class. Swaminathan slunk to his seat with a red face.

It was the English period presided over by Vedanayagam. He was reading the story of the old man who planted trees for posterity and was paid ten rupees by a king. Not a word reached Swaminathan's brain, in which there was only dull pain and vacuity. If he had been questioned he would have blundered and would have had to spend the rest of the hour standing on the bench. But his luck was good.

The period was over. He was walking home alone, rather slowly, with a troubled heart. Somu was going a few yards in front of him. Swaminathan cried out: "Somu, Somu...Somu, won't you stop?" Somu stopped till the other came up.

After a brief silence Swaminathan quavered: "What is the matter with you fellows?"

"Nothing very particular," replied Somu. "By the way, may I inform you that you have earned a new name? The Tail—Rajam's Tail, to be more precise. We aren't good enough for you, I believe. But how can everyone be a son of a police superintendent?" With that he was off.

This was probably Swaminathan's first shock in life. It paralysed all his mental process. When his mind started working again, he faintly wondered if he had been dreaming. The staid Somu, the genial Somu, the uncle Somu, was it the same Somu that had talked to him a few minutes ago? What was wrong in liking and going about with Rajam? Why did it make them so angry?

He went home, flung his coat and cap and books on the table, gulped down the cold coffee that was waiting for him, and sat on the *pyol*, vacantly gazing into the dark intricacies of the gutter that adorned

Vinayaka Mudali Street. A dark volume of water was rushing along. Odd pieces of paper, leaves, and sticks floated by. A small piece of tin was gently skimming along. Swaminathan had an impulse to plunge his hand in and pick it up. But he let it go. His mind was inert. He watched the shining bit float away. It was now at the end of the compound wall; now it had passed under the tree. Swaminathan was slightly irritated when a brick obstructed the progress of the tin. He said that the brick must either move along or stand aside without interfering with the traffic. The piece of tin released itself and dashed along furiously, disappearing round a bend at the end of the street. Swaminathan ran in, got a sheet of paper, and made a boat. He saw a small ant moving about aimlessly. He carefully caught it, placed it in the boat, and lowered the boat into the stream. He watched in rapture its quick motion. He held his breath when the boat with its cargo neared a danger zone formed by stuck up bits of straw and other odds and ends. The boat made a beautiful swerve to the right and avoided destruction. It went on and on. It neared a fatal spot where the waters were swirling round and round in eddies. Swaminathan was certain that his boat was nearing its last moment. He had no doubt that it was going to be drawn right to the bottom of the circling eddies. The boat whirled madly round, shaking and swaying and quivering. Providentially a fresh supply of water from the kitchen in the neighbour's house pushed it from behind out of danger. But it rushed on at a fearful speed, and Swaminathan felt that it was going to turn turtle. Presently it calmed, and resumed a normal speed. But when it passed under a tree, a thick dry leaf fell down and upset it. Swaminathan ran frantically to the spot to see if he could save at least the ant. He peered long into the water, but there was no sign of the ant. The boat and its cargo were wrecked beyond recovery. He took a pinch of earth, uttered a prayer for the soul of the ant, and dropped it into the gutter.

✳✳✳

In a few days Swaminathan got accustomed to his position as the enemy of Somu and company.

All the same, now and then he had an irresistible desire to talk to his old friends. When the scripture master pursed his lips and scratched his nose, Swaminathan had a wild impulse to stamp on the Pea's leg and laugh, for that was a joke that they had never failed to enjoy day after day for many years past. But now Swaminathan smothered the impulse and chuckled at it himself, alone. And again, when the boy with the red cap nodded in his seat and woke up with a start every time his head sank down, Swaminathan wanted to whisper into the Pea's ear: "Look at that fellow, third on the first bench, red cap—now he is falling off again—" and giggle; but he merely bit his lips and kept quiet.

Somu was looking in his direction. Swaminathan thought that there was friendliness in his look. He felt a momentary ecstasy as he realized that Somu was willing to be friendly again. They stared at each other for a while, and just as Swaminathan was beginning to put on a sweet friendly look, Somu's expression hardened and he turned away.

Swaminathan was loitering in the compound. He heard familiar voices behind, turned round, and saw Somu, Sankar, and the Pea following him. Swaminathan wondered whether to stop and join them, or wait till they had passed and then go in the opposite direction. For it was awkward to be conscious of the stare of three pairs of hostile eyes behind one's ears. He believed that every minute movement of his body was being watched and commented on by the three followers. He felt that his gait was showing unfavourably in their eyes. He felt they were laughing at the way in which he carried his books. There was a slight itching on his nape; his hand almost rose, but he checked it, feeling that the scratching would be studiously watched by the six keen eyes.

He wanted to turn to his right and enter the school hall. But that would be construed as cowardice; they would certainly think that he was doing it to escape from them. He wanted to run away, but that would be no better. He wanted to turn back and get away in the opposite direction, but that would mean meeting them square in the face. So his only recourse was to keep on walking as best he could, not showing that he was conscious of his followers. The same fellows ten days ago, what they were! Now what formidable creatures they had turned out to be! Swaminathan was wonderstruck at the change.

It was becoming unendurable. He felt that his legs were taking a circular motion, and were twining round each other when he walked. It was too late to turn and dash into the school hall. He had passed it. Now he had only one way of escape. He must run. It was imperative. He tried a trick. He paused suddenly, turned this way and that, as if looking for something, and then cried aloud: "Oh, I have left my notebook somewhere," raised his hand and was off from the spot like a stag.

5

FATHER'S ROOM

It was Saturday and Rajam had promised to come in the afternoon. Swaminathan was greatly excited. Where was he to entertain him? Probably in his own 'room'; but his father often came in to dress and undress. No, he would be at court, Swaminathan reminded himself with relief. He cleaned his table and arranged his books so neatly that his father was surprised and had a good word to say about it. Swaminathan went to his grandmother. "Granny," he said, "I have talked to you about Rajam, haven't I?"

"Yes. That boy who is very strong but never passes his examination."

"No. No. That is Mani."

"Oh, now I remember, it is a boy who is called the Gramme or something, that witty little boy."

Swaminathan made a gesture of despair. "Look here Granny, you are again mistaking the Pea for him. I mean Rajam, who has killed tigers, whose father is the Police Superintendent, and who is great."

"Oh," Granny cried, "that boy, is he coming here? I am so glad."

"H'm... But I have got to tell you—"

"Will you bring him to me? I want to see him."

"Let us see," Swaminathan said vaguely. "I can't promise. But I have got to tell you, when he is with me you must not call me or come to my room."

"Why so?" asked Granny.

"The fact is, you are—well, you are too old," said Swaminathan with brutal candour. Granny accepted her lot cheerfully.

That he must give his friend something very nice to eat, haunted his mind. He went to his mother, who was squatting before a cutter with a bundle of plantain leaves beside her. He sat before her, nervously crushing a piece of leaf this way and that, and tearing it to minute bits.

"Don't throw all those bits on the floor. I simply can't sweep the floor any more," she said.

"Mother, what are you preparing for the afternoon tiffin?"

"Time enough to think of it," said Mother.

"You had better prepare something very nice, something fine and sweet. Rajam is coming this afternoon. Don't make the sort of coffee that you usually give me. It must be very good and hot." He remembered how in Rajam's house everything was brought to the room by the cook. "Mother, would you mind if I don't come here for coffee and tiffin? Can you send it to my room?" He turned to the cook and said: "Look here, you can't come to my room in that *dhoti*. You will have to wear a clean, white *dhoti* and shirt." After a while he said: "Mother, can you ask Father to lend me his room for just an hour or two?" She said that she could not as she was very busy. Why could he himself not go and ask?

"Oh, he will give more readily if you ask," said Swaminathan.

He went to his father and said: "Father, I want to ask you something." Father looked up from the papers over which he was bent.

"Father, I want your room."

"What for?"

"I have to receive a friend," Swaminathan replied.

"You have your own room," Father said.

"I can't show it to Rajam."

"Who is this Rajam, such a big man?"

"He is the Police Superintendent's son. He is—he is not ordinary."

"I see. Oh! Yes, you can have my room, but be sure not to mess up the things on the table."

"Oh, I will be very careful. You are a nice father, Father."

Father guffawed and said: "Now run in, boy, and sit at your books."

***

Rajam's visit went off much more smoothly than Swaminathan had anticipated. Father had left his room open; Mother had prepared some marvel with wheat, plum, and sugar. Coffee was really good. Granny had kept her promise and did not show her senile self to Rajam. Swaminathan was only sorry that the cook did not change his *dhoti*.

Swaminathan seated Rajam in his father's revolving chair. It was nearly three hours since he had come. They had talked out all subjects—Mani, Ebenezar, trains, tiger-hunting, police, and ghosts.

"Which is your room?" Rajam asked.

Swaminathan replied with a grave face: "This is my room, why?"

Rajam took time to swallow this. "Do you read such books?" he asked, eyeing the big gilt-edged law books on the table. Swaminathan was embarrassed.

Rajam made matters worse with another question. "But where are your books?" There was just a flicker of a smile on his lips.

"The fact is," said Swaminathan, "this table belongs to my father. When I am out, he meets his clients in this room."

"But where do you keep your books?"

Swaminathan made desperate attempts to change the topic: "You have seen my grandmother, Rajam?"

"No. Will you show her to me? I should love to see her," replied Rajam.

"Wait a minute then," said Swaminathan and ran out. He had one last hope that his granny might be asleep. It was infinitely safer to show one's friends a sleeping granny.

He saw her sitting on her bed complacently. He was disappointed. He stood staring at her, lost in thought.

"What is it, boy?" Granny asked. "Do you want anything?"

"No. Aren't you asleep? Granny," he said a few minutes later, "I have brought Rajam to see you."

"Have you?" cried Granny. "Come nearer, Rajam. I can't see your face well. You know I am old and blind."

Swaminathan was furious and muttered under his breath that his granny had no business to talk all this drivel to Rajam.

Rajam sat on her bed. Granny stroked his hair and said that he had fine soft hair, though it was really short and prickly. Granny asked what his mother's name was, and how many children she had. She then asked if she had many jewels. Rajam replied that his mother had a black trunk filled with jewels, and a green one containing gold and silver vessels. Rajam then described to her Madras, its lighthouse, its sea, its trams and buses, and its cinemas. Every item made Granny gasp with wonder.

✳✳✳

When Swaminathan entered the class, a giggle went round the benches. He walked to his seat hoping that he might not be the cause of the giggling. But it continued. He looked about. His eyes travelled up to the blackboard. His face burnt red. On the board was written in huge letters TAIL. Swaminathan walked to the blackboard and rubbed it off with his hands. He turned and saw Sankar's head bent over his notebook, and the Pea was busy unpacking his satchel. Without a word Swaminathan approached the Pea and gave him a fierce slap on his cheek. The Pea burst into tears and swore that he did not do it. He cast a sly look at Sankar, who was absorbed in some work. Swaminathan turned to him and slapped his face also.

Soon there was pandemonium: Sankar, Swaminathan, and the Pea rolling over, tearing, scratching, and kicking one another. The bell rang. Rajam, Somu, and Mani entered. The teacher came in and stood aghast. He could do little more than look on and ejaculate. He was the old Tamil *pundit*, the most helpless teacher in the school.

Somu and Mani parted the fighters. The teacher ascended the platform and took his seat. The class settled down.

Somu got up and said: "Sir, please let us go out. We do not want to disturb the class."

The teacher demurred; but already Mani had gone out, pushing Swaminathan and the Pea before him. Somu followed him with Sankar.

They came to a lonely spot in the field adjoining the school. There was tense silence for a while, and Mani broke it: "What is wrong with you, you little rogues?"

Three started to speak at once. Swaminathan's voice was the loudest: "He—the Pea—wrote TAIL—Big Tail—on the blackboard—big—"

"No—I didn't, you—" screamed the Pea.

"The other too wrote it," cried Swaminathan pointing at Sankar.

"Rascal! Did you see me?" howled Sankar.

Mani covered their mouths with his hands. "What is a tail, anyway?" he asked, not having been told anything about it till then.

"They call me Rajam's tail," sobbed Swaminathan.

A frozen expression came over Mani's face, and he asked, "And who dares to talk of Rajam here?"

"Oh, dare!" repeated Somu.

"If any of you fellows have done it—" growled Mani looking at the trembling Sankar and the Pea.

"If they have, what can you do?" asked Somu with a contemptuous smile.

"What do you mean, Somu, what do you mean?"

"Look here, Mani," Somu cried, "for a long time I have been waiting to tell you this: you think too much of yourself and your powers."

Mani swung his hand and brought it down on Somu's nape. Somu pushed it away with a heavy blow. Mani aimed a kick at Somu, which would send him rolling. Somu stepped aside and delivered one himself, which nearly bent the other.

The three youngsters could hardly believe their eyes. Somu and Mani fighting! They lost their heads. They thought that Somu and Mani were killing each other. They looked accusingly at one another, and then ran towards the school.

They burst in upon the headmaster, who gathered from them with difficulty that in the adjacent field two murders were being committed at that very moment. He was disposed to laugh at first. But the excitement and seriousness on the boys' faces made him check his laughter and scratch his chin. He called a peon and with him set off to the field.

The fighters, rolling and rolling, were everywhere in the field. The headmaster and the peon easily picked them apart, much to the astonishment of Swaminathan, who had thought till then that the strength that Somu or Mani possessed was not possessed by anyone else in the world.

6

A FRIEND IN NEED

One afternoon three weeks later, Swaminathan stood before Mani's house and gave a low whistle. Mani joined him. They started for Rajam's house, speculating on the way about the surprise which Rajam had said he would give them if they saw him that afternoon.

"I think," said Swaminathan, "Rajam is merely joking. It is merely a trick to get us to his house." He was very nearly pushed into a gutter for this doubt.

"Probably he has bought a monkey or something," Swaminathan ventured again. Mani was gracious enough to admit that it might be so. They thought of all possible subjects that might surprise them, and gave up the attempt in the end.

Their thoughts turned to their enemies. "You know what I am going to do?" Mani asked. "I am going to break Somu's waist. I know where he lives. He lives in Kabir Street behind the market. I have often seen him coming out at nights to a shop in the market for *betel* leaves. I shall first fling a stone at the municipal lamp and put it out. You have no idea how dark Kabir Street is…I shall wait with my club, and as soon as he appears—He will sprawl in the dust with broken bones…" Swaminathan shuddered at the thought. "And that is not all," said Mani, "I am going to get that Pea under my heel and press him to the earth. And Sankar is going to hang by his tuft over Sarayu, from a *peepul* branch…"

They stopped talking when they reached Rajam's house. The gate was bolted, and they got up the wall and jumped in. A servant came running towards them. He asked, "Why did you climb the wall?"

"Is the wall your property?" Mani asked and burst into laughter.

"But if you had broken your ribs—" the servant began.

"What is that to you? Your ribs are safe, are they not?" Swaminathan asked ungraciously and laughed.

"And just a word more," Mani said, "do you happen to be by any chance the Police Superintendent's son?"

"No, no," replied the servant.

"Very well then," replied Mani, "we have come to see and talk to the Police Superintendent's son." The servant beat a hasty retreat.

They banged their fists on Rajam's door. They heard the clicking of the latch and hid themselves behind the pillar. Rajam peeped out and shut the door again.

They came out, stood before the door, and wondered what to do. Swaminathan applied his mouth to the keyhole and mewed like a cat. Mani pulled him away and putting his mouth to the hole barked like a dog. The latch clicked again, and the door slightly opened. Mani whispered to Swaminathan, "You are a blind kitten, I will be a blind puppy."

Mani fell down on his knees and hands, shut his eyes tight, pushed the door with his head, and entered Rajam's room in the role of a blind puppy. Swaminathan crawled behind him with shut eyes, mewing for all he was worth. They moved round and round the room, Rajam adding to the interest of the game by mewing and barking in answer every few seconds. The blind puppy brushed its side against a leg, and thinking that it belonged to Rajam softly bit the calf muscle. Imagine its confusion when it opened its eyes and saw that it was biting its enemy, Somu! The blind kitten nestled close to a leg and scratched it with its paw. Opening its eyes it found that it was fondling a leg that belonged to its enemy, Sankar.

Mani remained stunned for a moment, and then scrambled to his feet. He looked around, his face twitching with shame and rage. He saw the Pea sitting in a corner, his eyes twinkling with mischief, and felt impelled to take him by the throat. He turned round and saw Rajam regarding him steadily, his mouth still quivering with a smothered grin.

As for Swaminathan, he felt that the best place for himself would be the darkness and obscurity under a table or a chair.

"What do you mean by this, Rajam?" Mani asked.

"Why are you so wild?"

"It was your fault," said Mani vehemently, "I didn't know—" He looked around.

"Well, well. I didn't ask you to crawl and bark, did I?"

Somu and company laughed. Mani glared round, "I am going away, Rajam. This is not the place for me."

Rajam replied, "You may go away, if you don't want me to see you or speak to you any more."

Mani fidgeted uneasily. Rajam took him aside and soothed him. Rajam then turned to Swaminathan, who was lost in bottomless misery. He comforted and flattered him by saying that it was the best imitation of a cat and dog that he had ever witnessed in his life. He admitted that for a few minutes he wondered whether he was watching a real cat and a dog. They would get prizes if they did it in fairs. If Swaminathan and Mani would be good enough to repeat the fun, he would be delighted, and even ask his father to come and watch.

This was soothing. Swaminathan and Mani felt proud of themselves. And after the round of eating that followed, they were perfectly happy, except when they thought of the other three in the room.

They were in this state of mind when Rajam began a lecture on friendship. He said impressive things about friendship, quoting from his book the story of the dying old man and the faggots, which proved that union was strength. A friend in need was a friend indeed. He then started giving hair-raising accounts of what hell had in store for persons who fostered enmity. According to Rajam, it was written in the *Vedas* that a person who fostered enmity should be locked up in a small room, after his death. He would be made to stand, stark naked, on a pedestal of red-hot iron. There were beehives all around with bees as big as lemons. If the sinner stepped down from the pedestal, he would have to put his foot on immense scorpions and centipedes that crawled about the room in hundreds...

A shudder went through the company.

... The sinner would have to stand thus for a month, without food or sleep. At the end of a month he would be transferred to another place, a very narrow bridge over a lake of boiling oil. The bridge was so narrow that he would be able to keep only one foot on it at a time. Even on the narrow bridge there were plenty of wasp nests and cactus, and he would be goaded from behind to move on. He would have to balance on one foot and then on another, for ages and ages, to keep himself from falling into the steaming lake below, and move on indefinitely...

The company was greatly impressed. Rajam then invited everyone to come forward and say that they would have no more enemies. If Sankar said it, he would get a bound notebook; if Swaminathan said it, he would get a clockwork engine; if Somu said it, he would get a belt; and if Mani said it, he would get a nice pocket-knife; and the Pea would get a marvellous little pen.

He threw open the cupboard and displayed the prizes. There was silence for some time as each sat gnawing his nails. Rajam was sweating with his peacemaking efforts.

The Pea was the first to rise. He stood before the cupboard and said, "Let me see the fountain-pen." Rajam gave it to him. The Pea turned it round and round and gave it back without any comment. "Why, don't you like it?" Rajam asked. The Pea kept staring into the cupboard and said, "Can I have that box?" He pointed at a tiny box with a lot of yellow and black designs on it and a miniature Taj Mahal on its lid. Rajam said, "I can't give you that. I want it." He paused. He had two more boxes like that in his trunk. He changed his mind. "No. I don't want it. You can take the box if you like."

In a short while, Mani was sharpening a knife on his palm; Somu was trying a belt on; Sankar was fingering a thick bound notebook; and Swaminathan was jealously clasping a green engine to his bosom.

7

A New Arrival

Mother had been abed for two days past. Swaminathan missed her very much in the kitchen, and felt uncomfortable without her attentions. He was taken to her room, where he saw her lying dishevelled and pale on her bed. She asked him to come nearer. She asked him why he was looking emaciated and if he was not eating and sleeping well. Swaminathan kept staring at her blankly. Here seemed to be a different Mother. He was cold and reserved when he spoke to her. Her appearance depressed him. He wriggled himself from her grasp and ran out.

His granny told him that he was going to have a brother. He received the news without enthusiasm.

That night he was allowed to sleep on Granny's bed. The lights kept burning all night. Whenever he opened his eyes, he was conscious of busy feet scurrying along the passage. Late at night Swaminathan woke up and saw a lady doctor in the hall. She behaved as if the house belonged to her. She entered Mother's room, and presently out of the room came a mingled noise of whispers and stifled moans. She came out of the room with a serious face and ordered everybody about. She commanded even Father to do something. He vanished for a moment and reappeared with a small bottle in his hand. He hovered about uncertainly. The hushed voices, hurry, seriousness, agitation, hot water, and medicine—preparations for ushering a new person into the world—were too bewildering for Swaminathan's comprehension. Meanwhile Granny kept asking something of everybody that passed by, and no one troubled to answer her.

What did it matter? The five carpets in Granny's bed were cosy; her five pillows were snug; and Granny's presence nearby was reassuring; and above all, his eyelids were becoming heavy. What more did he want? He fell asleep.

***

The Tamil *pundit,* with his unshaven face and the silver-rimmed spectacles set askew on his nose, was guiding the class through the intricacies of Tamil grammar. The guide was more enthusiastic than his followers. A continual buzz filled the air. Boys had formed themselves into small groups and carried on private conversations. The *pundit* made faint attempts to silence the class by rapping his palms on the table.

After a while, he gave up the attempt and went on with his lecture. His voice was scarcely audible.

Sankar and a few others sat on the first bench with cocked-up ears and busy pencils.

Swaminathan and the Pea sat on the last bench.

"I say, Pea," said Swaminathan, "I got a new brother this morning."

The Pea was interested. "How do you like him?"

"Oh, like him! He is hardly anything. Such a funny-looking creature!" said Swaminathan and gave what he thought was an imitation of his little brother: he shut his eyes, compressed his lips, folded his hands on his chest, protruded his tongue, and tilted his head from side to side. The Pea laughed uncontrollably. "But," Swaminathan said, "this thing has a wonderful pair of hands, so small and plump, you know! But I tell you, his face is awful, red, red like chilli."

They listened to the teacher's lecture for a few minutes. "I say, Swami," said the Pea, "these things grow up soon. I have seen a baby that was just what your brother is. But you know, when I saw it again during Michaelmas I could hardly recognize it."

8

Before the Examinations

In April, just two weeks before the examinations, Swaminathan realized that his father was changing—for the worse. He was becoming fussy and difficult. He seemed all of a sudden to have made up his mind to harass his son. If the latter was seen chatting with his granny, he was told sourly, "Remember, boy, there is an examination. Your granny can wait, not your examination." If he was seen wandering behind his mother, he was hunted down and sent to his desk. If his voice was heard anywhere after the *Taluk* Office gong had struck nine, a command would come from his father's room, "Swami, why haven't you gone to bed yet? You must get up early and study a bit." This was a trying period in Swaminathan's life. One day he was piqued enough to retort, "Why are you so nervous about my examination?"

"Suppose you fail?"

"I won't."

"Of course you won't if you study hard and answer well...Suppose you fail and all your class-mates go up, leaving you behind? You can start doing just what you like on the very day your examination closes."

Swaminathan reflected: suppose the Pea, Mani, Rajam and Sankar deserted him and occupied Second Form A? His father was right. And then his father drove home the point. "Suppose all your juniors in the Fifth Standard become your class-mates?"

Swaminathan sat at decimals for half an hour.

***

At school everybody seemed to be overwhelmed by the thought of the examinations. It was weeks since anybody had seen a smile on Sankar's face. Somu had become brisk and businesslike. The Pea took time to grasp jokes, and seldom gave out any. And as for Rajam, he came to the school at the stroke of the first bell, took down everything the teacher said, and left at the stroke of the last bell, hardly uttering a dozen words to anybody. Mani was beginning to look worried and took every opportunity to take Sankar aside so as to clear the doubts that arose from time to time as he plodded through his texts. He dogged the steps of the school clerk. There was a general belief in the school that the clerk was omniscient and knew all the question papers of all the classes.

One day Mani went to the clerk's house and laid a neat bundle containing fresh brinjals at his feet. The clerk was pleased and took Mani in and seated him on a stool.

The clerk looked extremely amiable and Mani felt that he could ask anything at that moment and get it. The clerk was murmuring something about his cat, a lank ill-fed thing, that was nestling close to him. Most of what he was saying did not enter Mani's head. He was waiting feverishly to open the topic of question papers. The clerk had meanwhile passed from cats to eye-flies; but it made little difference to Mani, who was waiting for the other to pause for breath to launch his attack. "You must never let these eye-flies buzz near your eyes. All cases of eyesore can be traced to it. When you get eyesore the only thing you can do is to take a slice of raw onion..."

Mani realized that the other would not stop, and butted in. "There is only a week more for the examinations, sir..."

The clerk was slightly puzzled: "Yes, indeed, a week more...You must take care to choose only the juicy variety, the large juicy variety, not the small onion..."

"Sir," Mani interrupted, ignoring the juicy variety, "I am much worried about my examination." He tried to look pathetic.

"I am glad. If you read well, you will pass," said the Oracle.

"You see, sir, I am so worried, I don't sleep at nights, thinking of the examination...If you could possibly tell me something important...I have such a lot to study—don't want to study unnecessary things that may not be necessary for the examination." He meandered thus. The clerk understood what he was driving at, but said, "Just read all your portions and you will pass." Mani realized that diplomacy was not his line. He asked bluntly, "Please tell me, sir, what questions we are getting for our examination."

The clerk denied having any knowledge of the question papers. Mani flattered him by asking, if he did not know the questions, who else would. By just a little more of the same judicious flattery the clerk was moved to give what Mani believed to be valuable hints. In spite of the fact that he did not know what the First Form texts were, the clerk ventured to advise, "You must pay particular attention to geography. Maybe you will have to practise map-drawing a lot. And in arithmetic make it a point to solve at least five problems every day, and you will be able to tackle arithmetic as easily as you swallow plantains."

"And what about English?"

"Oh, don't worry about that. Have you read all your lessons?"

"Yes, sir," Mani replied without conviction.

"It is all right then. You must read all the important lessons again, and if you have time, yet again, and that will be ample."

These answers satisfied Mani greatly. On his way home, he smiled to himself and said that the four *annas* he had invested on brinjals was not after all a waste.

***

Mani felt important. He secretly pitied his classmates, who had to do work coolly without valuable hints to lighten their labour. He felt he ought to share his good secret with Swaminathan without divulging the source.

They were going home from the school. They stopped for a while at the junction of Vinayak Mudali and Grove Streets before parting ways. Mani said, "Young man, have you any idea what we are getting for the examination?"

"Nothing outside the covers of the textbooks."

Mani ignored the humour. "Now listen to me carefully: last night from seven to ten, do you know what I did?"

"Munched ground-nuts?"

"Idiot, don't joke. I made two maps of India, two of Africa, and one map of Europe."

"Say all the maps in the atlas."

"Maybe," Mani said, not quite liking the remark, "but I do it with some definite purpose…It may be that I know one or two questions. But don't let the other fellows know anything about it. I may get into trouble." Swaminathan was taken in by the other's seriousness and inferred a moral.

***

Reaching home, Swaminathan felt rather dull. His mother was not at home. Granny was not in a talkative mood. He related to her some exciting incidents of the day: "Granny, guess what happened in our school today. A boy in First Form C stabbed another in the forearm with a penknife."

"What for?" asked Granny mechanically.

"They were enemies." Finding that it fell flat, he brought out the big event of the day. "Granny, Granny, here is another thing. The headmaster knocked his toe against a door-post and oh! there was such a lot of blood! He went limping about the school the whole day. He couldn't take the Third Form and so they had leave, the lucky fellows!"

"Is it?" asked Granny.

Swaminathan perceived, to his intense disgust, that his granny was in one of her dull sleepy moods.

He strayed near the swing-cradle of his little brother. Though at first he had been sceptical of his brother's attractions and possibilities, now day by day he was finding him more interesting. This little one was now six months old and was charming. His attainments were: he made shrill noises whenever he saw anybody; thrust his fists into his mouth and damped his round arms up to the elbow; vigorously kicked the air; and frequently displayed his bare red gums in a smile. Swaminathan loved every inch of him. He would spend hours balancing himself on the edge of the cradle and trying to make him say 'Swaminathan'. The little one would gurgle, and Swaminathan would shriek, pretending that it was the other's futile version of his name.

Now he peered in and was disappointed to find the baby asleep. He cleared his throat aloud and coughed in the hope of waking him. But the baby slept. He waited for a moment, and tiptoed away, reminding himself that it was best to leave the other alone, as he had a knack of throwing the house in turmoil for the first half-hour whenever he awoke from sleep.

Staying at home in the evenings was extremely irksome. He sighed at the thought of the sandbanks of Sarayu and Mani's company. But his father had forbidden him to go out till the examinations were over. He often felt he ought to tell his father what he thought of him. But somehow when one came near doing it, one failed. He would have to endure it after all only for a week...The thought that he would have to put up with his travails only for a week at worst gave him fresh energy.

He sat at his table and took out his atlas. He opened the political map of Europe and sat gazing at it. It puzzled him how people managed to live in such a crooked country as Europe. He wondered what the shape of the people might be who lived in places where the outline narrowed as in a cape, and how they managed to escape being strangled by the contour of their land. And then another favourite problem began to tease him: how did those map-makers find out what the shape of a country was? How did they find out that Europe was like a camel's head? Probably they stood on high towers and copied what they saw below. He wondered if he would be able to see India as it looked in the map, if he stood on the top of the town hall. He had never been there nor ever did he wish to go there. Though he was incredulous, tailor Ranga persistently informed him that there was a torture chamber in the top story of the town hall to which *Pathans* decoyed young people.

He shook himself from his brown study and copied the map of Europe. He kept the original and his own copy side by side and congratulated himself on his ability to draw, though his outline looked like some strange animal that had part bull's face and part camel's.

It was past seven by now and his father came home. He was greatly pleased to see his son at work. "That is right, boy," he said looking at the map. Swaminathan felt that that moment was worth all his suffering. He turned over the pages and opened out the map of Africa.

***

Two days before his examination he sat down to draw up a list of his needs. On a piece of paper he wrote:

Unruled white paper	20 sheets
Nibs	6
Ink	2 bottles
Clips	
Pins	

He nibbled his pencil and reread the list. The list was disappointing. He had never known that his wants were so few. When he first sat down to draw the list he had hoped to fill two or three imposing pages. But now the cold lines on the paper numbered only five. He scrutinized the list again: 'Unruled white paper 20 sheets.' He asked himself why he was so particular about the paper's being unruled. It was a well-known fact that, try as he would, his lines had a tendency to curl up towards the right-hand corner of the paper. That would not do for examinations. He had better keep a stock of ruled paper. And then 'Nibs'. He wondered how many nibs one would need for an examination. One? Two? Five?...And then the Ink column worried him. How much of it did one buy? After that he had trouble with clips and pins. He not only had not the faintest idea of the quantity of each that he would need but was totally ignorant of the unit of purchase also. Could one go to a shop and demand six pins and six clips without offending the shopman?

At the end the list was corrected to:

Unruled white paper	20 sheets
Ruled white paper	10 sheets
Black ink	1 bottle
Clips	3—6—12
Pins	6—12

The list was not satisfactory even now. After pondering over it, he added 'Cardboard Pad One' and 'One Rupee For Additional Expenses'.

His father was busy in his office. Swaminathan stood before him with the list in his hand. Father was absorbed in his work and did not know that Swaminathan was there. Swaminathan suddenly realized that it would be better to approach his father at some other time. He could be sure of a better reception if he opened the question after food. He tiptoed out. When he was just outside the door, his father called out, "Who is that?" There was no friendliness in the tone. "Who is that I say?" roared Father again and was at his side with a scowling face before Swaminathan could decide whether to sneak out or stop and answer.

"Was it you?"

"Yes."

"You idiot, why couldn't you answer instead of driving me hoarse calling out "Who is that? Who is that?"...A man can't have peace in this house even for a second. Here I am at work—and every fifth second somebody or other pops in with some fool question or other. How am I to go on? Go and tell your mother that she can't come to my room for the rest of the day. I don't care if the whole battalion of oilmongers and vegetable women come and clamour for money. Let her drive them out. Your mother seems to think—what is that paper in your hand?"

"Nothing, Father," Swaminathan answered, thrusting the paper into his pocket.

"What is that?" Father shouted, snatching the list. Reading it with a terrific scowl, he went back to his chair. "What is this thing?"

Swaminathan had to cough twice to find his voice. "It is—my—examination list."

"What examination list?"

"My examinations begin the day after tomorrow, you know."

"And yet you are wandering about the house like an unleashed donkey! What preposterous list is this? Do you think rupees, *annas* and paise drop from the sky?"

Swaminathan did not think so, but something nearly so.

Father pulled out a drawer and peering into it said: "You can take from me anything you want. I haven't got clips. You don't need them. And then the pad, why do you want a pad? Are there no desks in your rooms? In our day slates were good enough for us. But now you want pen, paper, ink, and pad to keep under the paper..."

He took out an awful red pencil and scored out the 'Pad' from the list. It almost gashed the list. He flung it back at Swaminathan, who looked at it sadly. How deliciously he had been dreaming of going to Ameer Mart, jingling with coins, and buying things!

He was just going out when Father called him back and said: "Here, boy, as you go, for goodness' sake, remove the baby from the hall. I can't stand his idiotic cry...What is the matter with him?...Is your mother deaf or callous? The child may cry till he has fits, for aught she cares..."

9

SCHOOL BREAKS UP

With dry lips, parched throat, and ink-stained fingers, and exhaustion on one side and exaltation on the other, Swaminathan strode out of the examination hall on the last day.

Standing in the veranda, he turned back and looked into the hall and felt slightly uneasy. He would have felt more comfortable if all the boys had given their papers as he had done, twenty minutes before time. With his left shoulder resting against the wall, Sankar was lost to the world. Rajam, sitting under the second ventilator, between two third-form boys, had become a writing-machine. Mani was still gazing at the rafters, scratching his chin with the pen. The Pea was leaning back in his seat, revising his answers. One supervisor was drowsing in his chair; another was pacing up and down with an abstracted look in his eyes. The scratchy noise of active nibs, the rustle of papers, and the clearing of the throats, came through the brooding silence of the hall.

Swaminathan suddenly wished that he had not come out so soon. But how could he have stayed in the hall longer? The Tamil paper was set to go on till five o'clock. He had found himself writing the last line of the last question at four-thirty. Out of the six questions set, he had answered the first question to his satisfaction, the second was doubtful, the third was satisfactory, the fourth he knew was clearly wrong (but then, he did not know the correct answer).

The sixth answer was the best of the lot. It took only a minute to answer it. He had read the question at two minutes to four-thirty, started answering a minute later, and finished it at four-thirty. The question was: "What moral do you infer from the story of the *Brahmin* and the Tiger?" (A *brahmin* was passing along the edge of a pond. A tiger hailed him from the other bank and offered him a gold bangle. The *brahmin* at first declined the offer, but when the tiger protested its innocence and sincerity and insisted upon his taking the bangle, he waded through the water. Before he could hold out his hand for the bangle, he was inside the tiger.)

Swaminathan had never thought that this story contained a moral. But now he felt that it must have one since the question paper mentioned it. He took a minute to decide whether the moral was: 'We must never accept a gold bangle when it is offered by a tiger' or 'Love of gold bangle cost one one's life'. He saw more logic in the latter and wrote it down. After writing, he had looked at the big hall clock. Half an hour more! What had he to do for half an hour? But he felt awkward to be the first to go out. Why could not the others be as quick and precise as he?

He had found it hard to kill time. Why wasn't the paper set for two and a half hours instead of three? He had looked wistfully at the veranda outside. If only he could pluck up enough courage to hand in the paper and go out—he would have no more examination for a long time to come—he could do what he pleased— roam about the town in the evenings and afternoons and mornings—throw away the books—command Granny to tell endless tales.

He had seen a supervisor observing him, and had at once pretended to be busy with the answer paper. He thought that while he was about it, he might as well do a little revision. He read a few lines of the first question and was bored. He turned over the leaves and kept gazing at the last answer. He had to pretend that he was revising. He kept gazing at the moral of the tiger story till it lost all its meaning. He set his pen to work. He went on improving the little dash under the last line indicating the end, till it became an elaborate complicated pattern.

He had looked at the clock again, thinking that it must be nearly five now. It was only ten minutes past four-thirty. He saw two or three boys giving up their papers and going out, and felt happy. He briskly folded the paper and wrote on the flap the elaborate inscription:

> Tamil   Tamil
>
> W. S. Swaminathan
>
> 1st Form A section
>
> Albert Mission School
>
> Malgudi
>
> South India
>
> Asia.

The bell rang. In twos and threes boys came out of the hall. It was a thorough contrast to the preceding three hours. There was the din of excited chatter.

"What have you written for the last question?" Swaminathan asked a class-mate.

"Which? The moral question?...Don't you remember what the teacher said in the class?...'Love of gold cost the *brahmin* his life.'"

"Where was gold there?" Swaminathan objected. "There was only a gold bangle. How much have you written for the question?"

"One page," said the class-mate.

Swaminathan did not like this answer. He had written only a line. "What! You should not have written so much."

A little later he found Rajam and Sankar. "Well, boys, how did you find the paper?"

"How did you find it?" Sankar asked.

"Not bad," Swaminathan said.

"I was afraid only of Tamil," said Rajam, "now I think I am safe. I think I may get passing marks."

"No. Certainly more. A class," Sankar said.

"Look here," Swaminathan said, "some fools have written a page for that moral question."

"I wrote only three-quarters of a page," Rajam said.

"And I only a little more than half," said Sankar, who was an authority on these matters.

"I too wrote about that length, about half a page," lied Swaminathan as a salve to his conscience, and believed it for the moment.

"Boys, do you remember that we have no school from tomorrow?"

"Oh, I forgot all about it," Rajam said.

"Well, what are you going to do with yourselves?" somebody asked.

"I am going to use my books as fuel in the kitchen," Swaminathan said.

"My father has bought a lot of books for me to read during the vacation, *Sinbad the Sailor, Alibaba,* and so on," said Sankar.

Mani came throwing up his arms and wailing: "Time absolutely insufficient. I could have dashed off the last question."

The Pea appeared from somewhere with a huge streak of ink on his left cheek. "Hallo Sankar, first class?"

"No. May hardly get thirty-five."

"You rascal, you are lying. If you get a first class, may I cut off your tuft?" Mani asked.

The bell rang again fifteen minutes later. The whole school crowded into the hall. There was joy in every face and good fellowship in every word. Even the teachers tried to be familiar and pleasant. Ebenezar, when he saw Mani, asked: "Hallo, blockhead, how are you going to waste your vacation?"

"I am going to sleep, sir," Mani said, winking at his friends.

"Are you likely to improve your head by the time you return to the school?"

"How is it possible, sir, unless you cut off Sankar's head and present it to me?"

A great roar of laughter followed this. There would have been roars of laughter at anything; the mood was such. In sheer joy the drawing master was bringing down his cane on a row of feet because, he said, he saw some toes growing to an abnormal length.

The headmaster appeared on the platform, and after waiting for the noise to subside, began a short speech in which he said that the school would remain closed till the nineteenth of June and open again on the twentieth. He hoped that the boys would not waste their time but read story-books and keep glancing through the books prescribed for their next classes, to which, he hoped, most of them were going to be promoted. And now a minute more, there would be a prayer, after which the boys might disperse and go home.

At the end of the prayer the storm burst. With the loudest, lustiest cries, the gathering flooded out of the hall in one body. All through this vigorous confusion and disorder, Swaminathan kept close to Mani. For there was a general belief in the school that enemies stabbed each other on the last day. Swaminathan had no enemy as far as he could remember. But who could say? The school was a bad place.

Mani did some brisk work at the school gate, snatching from all sorts of people ink-bottles and pens, and destroying them. Around him was a crowd seething with excitement and joy. Ecstatic shrieks went up as each article of stationery was destroyed. One or two little boys feebly protested. But Mani wrenched the ink-bottles from their hands, tore their caps, and poured ink over their clothes. He had a small band of assistants, among whom Swaminathan was prominent. Overcome by the mood of the hour, he had spontaneously emptied his ink-bottle over his own head and had drawn frightful dark circles under his eyes with the dripping ink.

A policeman passed in the road. Mani shouted: "Oh, policeman, policeman! Arrest these boys!" A triumphant cry from a hundred throats rent the air. A few more ink-bottles exploded on the ground and a few more pens were broken. In the midst of it Mani cried: "Who will bring me Singaram's turban? I shall dye it for him."

Singaram, the school peon, was the only person who was not affected by the spirit of liberty that was abroad, and as soon as the offer to dye his turban reached his ears, he rushed into the crowd with a big stick and dispersed the revellers.

10

THE COACHMAN'S SON

Swaminathan had two different attachments: one to Somu, Sankar, and the Pea—a purely scholastic one, which automatically ceased when the school gates closed; his other attachment was more human, to Rajam and Mani. Now that they had no school, they were free from the shackles of time and were almost always together, and arranged for themselves a hectic vacation.

Swaminathan's one consuming passion in life now was to get a hoop. He dreamt of it day and night. He feasted on visions of an ex-cycle wheel without spokes or tyre. You had only to press a stick into the groove and the thing would fly. Oh, what joy to see it climb small obstacles, and how gently it took curves! When running it made a steady hum, which was music to the ear. Swaminathan thought that anybody in Malgudi would understand that he was coming, even a mile away, by that hum. He sometimes kept awake till ten-thirty in the night, thinking of this hoop. He begged everyone that he came across, from his father's friends to a municipal sweeper that he knew, to give him a cycle wheel. Now he could not set his eyes on a decent bicycle without his imagination running riot over its wheels. He dreamt one night that he crossed the Sarayu near Nallappa's Grove 'on' his wheel. It was a vivid dream: the steel wheel crunched on the sandy bed of the river as it struggled and heaved across. It became a sort of horse when it reached the other bank. It went back home in one leap, took him to the kitchen, and then to his bed, and lay down beside him. This was fantastic; but the early part of the dream was real enough. It nearly maddened him to wake to a hoopless morning.

In sheer despair he opened his heart to a coachman—a casual acquaintance of his. The coachman was very sympathetic. He agreed that existence was difficult without a hoop. He said that he would be able to give Swaminathan one in a few hours if the latter could give him five rupees. This was an immense sum, which Swaminathan hoped to possess in some distant future when he should become as tall as his father. He said so. At which the coachman gave a convincing talk on how to get it. He wanted only six paise to start with; in a short time he would make it six *annas*, and after that convert it to six rupees. And Swaminathan could spend the five out of the six rupees on the hoop and the balance of one rupee just as he pleased. Swaminathan declared that nothing would give him greater happiness than giving that extra rupee to the coachman. If any doubts arose in Swaminathan's mind, they were swept away by the other's rhetoric. The coachman's process of minting higher currency was this: he had a special metal pot at home in which he kept all base copper coins together with some mysterious herb (whose name he would not reveal even if he were threatened with torture). He kept the whole thing, he said, buried in the ground, he squatted on the spot at dead of night and performed some yoga, and lo when the time came, all the copper was silver. He could make even gold, but to get the herbs for it, he would have to walk two hundred and fifty miles across strange places, and he did not consider it worth all that exertion.

Swaminathan asked him when he might see him again as he had to think out and execute a plan to get six paise. The coachman said that if the other did not get the money immediately he would not be available for weeks to come as his master was going away and he would have to go away too. Swaminathan cringed and begged him to grant him six hours and ran home.

He first tried Granny. She almost shed tears that she had no money, and held her wooden box upside down to prove how hard up she was.

"I know, Granny, you have a lot of coins under your pillows."

"No, boy. You can search if you like."

Swaminathan ordered Granny to leave the bed and made a thorough search under the pillows and the carpets.

"Why do you want money now?" Granny asked.

"If you have what I want, have the goodness to oblige me. If not, why ask futile questions?"

Granny cried to Mother: "If you have money, give this boy six paise." But nobody was prepared to oblige Swaminathan. Father dismissed the request in less than a second, which made Swaminathan wonder what he did with all the money that he took from his clients.

He now tried a last desperate chance. He fell on his hands and knees and, resting his cheek on the cold cement floor, peered into the dark space under his father's heavy wardrobe. He had a wild notion that he might find a few coins scattered there. He thrust his hand under the wardrobe and moved it in all directions. All that he was able to collect was a disused envelope musty with cobweb and dust, a cockroach, and pinches of fine dust.

He sometimes believed that he could perform magic, if only he set about it with sufficient earnestness. He also remembered Ebenezar's saying in the class that God would readily help those that prayed to him.

He secured a small cardboard box, placed in it a couple of pebbles, and covered them with fine sand and leaves. He carried the box to the *pooja* room and placed it in a corner. It was a small room in which a few framed pictures of gods hung on the wall, and a few bronze and brass idols kept staring at Swaminathan from a small carved wooden pedestal. A permanent smell of flowers, camphor, and incense hung in the air.

Swaminathan stood before the gods and with great piety informed them of the box and its contents, how he expected them to convert the two pebbles into two three-paise coins, and why he needed money so urgently. He promised that if the gods helped him, he would give up biting his thumb. He closed his eyes and muttered: "Oh, *Sri Rama!* Thou hast slain *Ravana* though he had ten heads, can't you give me six paise?... If I give you the six paise now, when will you give me the hoop? I wish you would tell me what that herb is...Mani, shall I tell you the secret of getting a hoop? Oh, *Rama!* Give me six paise and I will give up biting my thumb for a year..."

He wandered aimlessly in the backyard persuading himself that in a few minutes he could return to the *pooja* room and take his money—transmuted pebbles. He fixed a time-limit of half an hour.

Ten minutes later he entered the *pooja* room, prostrated himself before the gods, rose, and snatching his box, ran to a secluded place in the backyard. With a fluttering heart he opened the box. He emptied it on the ground, ran his fingers through the mass of sand and leaves, and picked up the two pebbles. As he gazed at the cardboard box, the scattered leaves, sand, and the unconverted pebbles, he was filled with rage. The indifference of the gods infuriated him and brought tears to his eyes. He wanted to abuse the gods, but was afraid to. Instead, he vented all his rage on the cardboard box, and kicked it from place to place and stamped upon the leaves and sand. He paused and doubted if the gods would approve of even this. He was afraid that it might offend them. He might get on without money, but it was dangerous to incur the wrath of gods; they might make him fail in his examinations, or kill Father, Mother, Granny, or the baby. He picked up the box again and put back into it the sand, the leaves, and the pebbles that were crushed, crumpled, and kicked a minute ago. He dug a small pit at the root of a banana tree and buried the box reverently.

***

Ten minutes later he stood in Abu Lane, before Mani's house, and whistled twice or thrice. Mani did not appear. Swaminathan climbed the steps and knocked on the door. As the door-chain clanked inside, he stood in suspense. He was afraid he might not be able to explain his presence if anyone other than Mani should open the door. The door opened, and his heart sank. A big man with bushy eyebrows stood before him. "Who are you?" he asked.

"Who are you? Where is Mani?" Swaminathan asked. This was intended to convey that he had come to see Mani but was quite surprised to meet this other person, and would like to know who it was whom he had the pleasure of seeing before him. But in his confusion he could not put this sentiment in better form.

"You ask me who I am in my own house?" bellowed the Bushy-Eyebrows. Swaminathan turned and jumped down the steps to flee. But the Bushy-Eyebrows ordered: "Come here, little man." It was impossible to disobey this command. Swaminathan slowly advanced up the steps, his eyes bulging with terror. The Bushy-Eyebrows said: "Why do you run away? If you have come to see Mani, why don't you see him?" This was logic absolute.

"Never mind," Swaminathan said irrelevantly.

"Go in and see him, little man."

Swaminathan meekly entered the house. Mani was standing behind the door, tame and unimpressive in his domestic setting. He and Swaminathan stood staring at each other, neither of them uttering a single word. The Bushy-Eyebrows was standing in the doorway with his back to them, watching the street. Swaminathan pointed a timid finger and jerked his head questioningly. Mani whispered: "Uncle." The uncle suddenly turned round and said: "Why do you stand staring at each other? Did you come for that? Wag your tongues, boys." After this advice he stepped into the street to drive away two dogs that came and rolled in front of the house, locked in a terrible fight. He was now out of earshot.

Swaminathan said: "Your uncle? I never knew. I say, Mani, can't you come out now?...No?...I came on urgent business. Give me—urgent—six paise—got to have it—coachman goes away for weeks—may not get the chance again—don't know what to do without hoop..."

He paused. Mani's uncle was circling round the dogs, swearing at them and madly searching for stones.

Swaminathan continued: "My life depends on it. If you don't give it, I am undone. Quick, get the money."

"I have no money, nobody gives me money," Mani replied.

Swaminathan felt lost. "Where does your uncle keep his money? Look into that box..."

"I don't know."

"Mani, come here," his uncle cried from the street, "drive away these devils. Get me a stone."

✳✳✳

"Rajam, can you lend me a policeman?" Swaminathan asked two weeks later.

"Policeman! Why?"

"There is a rascal in this town who has robbed me." He related to Rajam his dealings with the coachman. "And now," he said, continuing his tale of woe, "whenever he sees me, he pretends not to recognize me. If I go to his house I am told he is not at home, though I can hear him cursing somebody inside. If I persist, he sends word that he will unchain his dog and kill me."

"Has he a dog?" asked Rajam.

"Not any that I could see."

"Then why not rush into his house and kick him?"

"It is all very well to say that. I tremble whenever I go to see him. There is no knowing what coachmen have in their houses... He may set his horse on me."

"Let him, it isn't going to eat you," said Mani.

"Isn't it? I am glad to know it. You come with me one day to tailor Ranga and hear what he has to say about horses. They are sometimes more dangerous than even tigers," Swaminathan said earnestly.

"Suppose you wait one day and catch him at the gate?" Rajam suggested.

"I have tried it. But whenever he comes out, he is on his coach. And as soon as he sees me, he takes out his long whip. I get out of his reach and shout. But what is the use? That horse simply flies! And to think that he has duped me of two *annas*!"

"It was six paise, wasn't it?"

"But he took from me twice again, six paise each time..."

"Then it is only an anna and a half," Rajam said.

"No, Rajam. It is two *annas*."

"My dear boy, twelve paise make an anna, and you have paid thrice, six paise each time; that is eighteen paise in all, one anna and a half."

"It is a useless discussion. Who cares how many paise make an anna?" Swaminathan said.

"But in money matters, you must be precise—very well, go on, Swami."

"The coachman first took from me six paise, promising me the silver coins in two days. He dodged me for four days and demanded six more paise, saying that he had collected herbs for twelve paise. He put me off again and took from me another six paise, saying that without it the whole process would fail. And after that, every time I went to him he put me off with some excuse or other; he often complained that owing to the weather the process was going on rather slowly. And two days ago he told me that he did not know me or anything about my money. And now you know how he behaves—I don't mind the money, but I hate his boy—that dark rascal. He makes faces at me whenever he sees me, and he has threatened to empty a bucketful of drain-water on my head. One day he held up an open penknife. I want to thrash him; that will make his father give me back my two *annas*."

***

Next day Swaminathan and Mani started for the coachman's house. Swaminathan was beginning to regret that he had ever opened the subject before his friends. The affair was growing beyond his control. And considering the interest that Rajam and Mani displayed in the affair, one could not foresee where it was going to take them all.

Rajam had formed a little plan to decoy and kidnap the coachman's son. Mani was his executive. He was to befriend the coachman's son. Swaminathan had very little part to play in the preliminary stages. His duty would cease with pointing out the coachman's house to Mani.

The coachman lived a mile from Swaminathan's house, westward in Keelacheri, which consisted of about a dozen thatched huts and dingy hovels, smoke-tinted and evil-smelling, clustering together irregularly.

They were now within a few yards of the place. Swaminathan tried a last desperate chance to stop the wheel of vengeance.

"Mani, I think the coachman's son has returned the money."

"What!"

"I think..."

"You think so, do you? Can you show it to me?"

Swaminathan pleaded: "Leave him alone, Mani. You don't know what troubles we shall get into by tampering with that boy..."

"Shut up or I will wring your neck."

"Oh, Mani—the police—or the boy himself—he is frightful, capable of anything." He had in his heart a great dread of the boy. And sometimes in the night would float before him a face dark, dirty and cruel, and make him shiver. It was the face of the coachman's son.

"He lives in the third house," Swaminathan pointed out.

At the last moment Mani changed his plan and insisted upon Swaminathan's following him to the coachman's house. Swaminathan sat down in the road as a protest. But Mani was stubborn. He dragged Swaminathan along till they came before the coachman's house, and then started shouting at him.

"Mani, Mani, what is the matter?"

"You son of a donkey," Mani roared at Swaminathan and swung his hand to strike him.

Swaminathan began to cry. Mani attempted to strangle him. A motley crowd gathered round them, urchins with prodigious bellies, women of dark aspect, and their men. Scurvy chickens cackled and ran hither and thither. The sun was unsparing. Two or three mongrels lay in the shade of a tree and snored. A general malodour of hencoop and unwashed clothes pervaded the place.

And now from the hovel that Swaminathan had pointed out as the coachman's, emerged a little man of three feet or so, ill-clad and unwashed. He pushed his way through the crowd and, securing a fine place, sucked his thumb and watched the fight in rapture. Mani addressed the crowd indignantly, pointing at Swaminathan: "This urchin, I don't know who he is, all of a sudden demands two *annas* from me. I have never seen him before. He says I owe him that money."

Mani continued in this strain for fifteen minutes. At the end of it, the coachman's son took the thumb out of his mouth and remarked: "He must be sent to the gaol." At this Mani bestowed an approving smile upon him and asked: "Will you help me to carry him to the police station?"

"No," said the coachman's son, being afraid of police stations himself.

Mani asked: "How do you know that he must be taken to the police station?"

"I know it."

"Does he ever trouble you similarly?" asked Mani.

"No," said the boy.

"Where is the two *annas* that your father took from me?" asked Swaminathan, turning to the boy his tear-drenched face. The crowd had meanwhile melted, after making half-hearted attempts to bring peace. Mani asked the boy suddenly: "Do you want this top?" He held a shining red top. The boy put out his hand for the top.

Mani said: "I can't give you this. If you come with me, I will give you a bigger one. Let us become friends."

The boy had no objection. "Won't you let me see it?" he asked. Mani gave it to him. The boy turned it in his hand twice or thrice and in the twinkling of an eye disappeared from the place. Mani took time to grasp the situation. When he did grasp it, he saw the boy entering a hovel far off. He started after him.

When Mani reached the hovel, the door was closed. Mani knocked a dozen times, before a surly man appeared and said that the boy was not there. The door was shut again. Mani started knocking again. Two or three menacing neighbours came round and threatened to bury him alive if he dared to trouble them in their own locality. Swaminathan was desperately appealing to Mani to come away. But it took a great deal more to move him. He went on knocking.

The neighbours took up their position a few yards off, with handfuls of stones, and woke the dogs sleeping under the tree.

It was only when the dogs came bouncing towards them that Mani shouted: "Run," to Swaminathan, and set an example himself.

A couple of stones hit Swaminathan on the back. One or two hit Mani also. A sharp stone skinned Mani's right heel. They became blind and insensible to everything except the stretch of road before them.

11

IN FATHER'S PRESENCE

During summer Malgudi was one of the most detested towns in South India. Sometimes the heat went above a hundred and ten in the shade, and between twelve and three any day in summer the dusty blanched roads were deserted. Even donkeys and dogs, the most vagrant of animals, preferred to move to the edge of the street, where catwalks and minor projections from buildings cast a sparse strip of shade, when the fierce sun tilted towards the west.

But there is this peculiarity about heat: it appears to affect only those that think of it. Swaminathan, Mani and Rajam would have been surprised if anybody had taken the trouble to prove to them that the Malgudi sun was unbearable. They found the noon and the afternoon the most fascinating part of the day. The same sun that beat down on the head of Mr Hentel, the mill manager, and drove him to Kodaikanal, or on the turban of Mr Krishnan, the Executive Engineer, and made him complain that his profession was one of the hardest, compelling him to wander in sun and storm, beat down on Swaminathan's curly head, Mani's tough matted hair, and Rajam's short wiry crop, and left them unmoved. The same sun that baked the earth so much that even Mr Retty, the most Indianized of the 'Europeans', who owned a rice mill in the deserted bungalow outside the town (he was, by the way, the mystery man of the place: nobody could say who he was or where he had come from; he swore at his boy and at his customers in perfect Tamil and always moved about in shirt, shorts, and sandalled feet) screamed one day when he forgetfully took a step or two barefoot—the same sun made the three friends loath to remain under a roof.

They were sitting on a short culvert, half a mile outside the municipal limits, on the trunk road. A streak of water ran under the culvert on a short stretch of sand, and mingled with Sarayu farther down. There was no tree where they sat, and the sun struck their heads directly. On the sides of the road there were paddy-fields; but now all that remained was scorched stubble, vast stretches of stubble, relieved here and there by clustering groves of mango or coconut. The trunk road was deserted but for an occasional country cart lumbering along.

"I wish you had done just what I had asked you to do and nothing more," said Rajam to Mani.

Swaminathan complained: "Yes, Rajam. I just showed him the coachman's son and was about to leave him, just as we had planned, when all of a sudden he tried to murder me..." He shot an angry glance at Mani.

Mani was forlorn. "Boys, I admit that I am an idiot. I thought I could do it all by the plan that came to my head on the spot. If I had only held the top firmly, I could have decoyed him, and by now he would have been howling in a lonely shed." There was regret in his tone.

Swaminathan said, nursing his nape: "It is still paining here." After the incident at Keelacheri, it took three hours of continuous argument for Mani to convince Swaminathan that the attack on him was only sham.

"You needn't have been so brutal to Swami," said Rajam.

"Sirs," Mani said, folding his hands, "I shall stand on my head for ten minutes, if you want me to do it as a punishment. I only pretended to scratch Swami to show the coachman's boy that I was his enemy."

A jingling was now heard. A close mat-covered cart drawn by a white bullock was coming down the road. When it had come within a yard of the culvert, they rose, advanced, stood in a row, and shouted: "Pull up the animal, will you?"

The cart driver was a little village boy.

"Stop the cart, you fool," cried Rajam.

"If he does not stop, we shall arrest him and confiscate his cart." This was Swaminathan.

The cart driver said: "Boys, why do you stop me?"

"Don't talk," Mani commanded, and with a serious face went round the cart and examined the wheels; he bent down and scrutinized the bottom of the cart. "Hey, cart man, get down."

"Boys, I must go," pleaded the driver.

"Whom do you address as 'boys'?" asked Rajam menacingly. "Don't you know who we are?"

"We are the Government Police out to catch humbugs like you," added Swaminathan.

"I shall shoot you if you say a word," said Rajam to the young driver. Though the driver was incredulous, he felt that there must be something in what they said.

Mani rapped a wheel and said: "The culvert is weak, we can't let you go over it unless you show us the pass."

The cart driver jabbered: "Please, sirs, let me—I have to be there."

"Shut up," Rajam commanded.

Swaminathan examined the animal and said: "Come here."

The cart driver was loath to get down. Mani dragged him from his seat and gave him a push towards Swaminathan.

Swaminathan scowled at him, and pointing at the sides of the animal, asked: "Why have you not washed the animal, you blockhead?"

The villager replied timidly: "I have washed the animal, sir."

"But why is this here?" Swaminathan asked, pointing at a brown patch.

"Oh, that! The animal has had it since its birth, sir."

"Birth? Are you trying to teach me?" Swaminathan shouted and raised his leg to kick the cart driver.

They showed signs of relenting.

"Give the rascal a pass, and be done with him," Rajam conceded graciously. Swaminathan took out a pencil stub and a grubby pocket-book that he always carried about him on principle. It was his habit to note down all sorts of things: the number of cycles that passed him, the number of people going barefoot, the number going with sandals or shoes on, and so forth.

He held the paper and pencil ready. Mani took hold of the rope of the bullock, pushed it back, and turned it the other way round. The cart driver protested. But Mani said: "Don't worry. It has got to stand here. This is the boundary."

"I have to go this way, sir."

"You can turn it round and go."

"What is your name?" asked Rajam.

"Karuppan," answered the boy.

Swaminathan took it down.

"Age?"

"I don't know, sir."

"You don't know? Swami, write a hundred," said Rajam.

"No sir, no sir, I am not a hundred."

"Mind your business and hold your tongue. You are a hundred. I will kill you if you say no. What is your bullock's name?"

"I don't know, sir."

"Swami, write 'Karuppan' again."

"Sir, that is my name, not the bullock's."

They ignored this and Swaminathan wrote 'Karuppan' against the name of the bullock.

"Where are you going?"

"Sethur."

Swaminathan wrote it down.

"How long will you stay there?"

"It is my place, sir."

"If that is so, what brought you here?"

"Our headman sent ten bags of coconut to the railway shed."

Swaminathan entered every word in his notebook. Then all the three signed the page, tore it off, gave it to the cart driver, and permitted him to start.

***

Much to Swaminathan's displeasure, his father's courts closed in the second week of May and Father began to spend the afternoons at home. Swaminathan feared that it might interfere with his afternoon rambles with Rajam and Mani. And it did. On the very third day of his vacation, Father commanded Swaminathan, just as he was stepping out of the house: "Swami, come here."

Father was standing in the small courtyard, wearing a *dhoti* and a *banian,* the dress which, for its very homeliness, Swaminathan detested to see him in; it indicated that he did not intend going out in the near future.

"Where are you going?"

"Nowhere."

"Where were you yesterday at this time?"

"Here."

"You are lying. You were not here yesterday. And you are not going out now."

"That is right," Mother added, just appearing from somewhere, "there is no limit to his loafing in the sun. He will die of sunstroke if he keeps on like this."

Father would have gone on even without Mother's encouragement. But now her words spurred him to action. Swaminathan was asked to follow him to his 'room' in his father's dressing-room.

"How many days is it since you have touched your books?" Father asked as he blew off the fine layer of dust on Swaminathan's books, and cleared the web that an industrious spider was weaving between a corner of the table and the pile of books.

Swaminathan viewed this question as a gross breach of promise.

"Should I read even when I have no school?"

"Do you think you have passed the B.A.?" Father asked.

"I mean, Father, when the school is closed, when there is no examination, even then should I read?"

"What a question! You must read."

"But Father, you said before the examinations that I needn't read after they were over. Even Rajam does not read." As he uttered the last sentence, he tried to believe it; he clearly remembered Rajam's complaining bitterly of a home tutor who came and pestered him for two hours a day thrice a week.

Father was apparently deaf to Swaminathan's remarks. He stood over Swaminathan and set him to dust his books and clean his table. Swaminathan vigorously started blowing off the dust from the book covers. He caught the spider carefully, and took it to the window to throw it out. He held it outside the window and watched it for a while. It was swinging from a strand that gleamed in a hundred delicate tints.

"Look sharp! Do you want a whole day to throw out the spider?" Father asked. Swaminathan suddenly realized that he might have the spider as his pet and that it would be a criminal waste to throw it out. He secretly slipped it into his pocket and, after shaking an empty hand outside the window, returned to his duty at the desk.

"Look at the way you have kept your English text! Are you not ashamed of yourself?" Swaminathan picked up the oily red-bound *Fourth Reader,* opened it, and banged together the covers in order to shake off the dust, and then rubbed violently the oily covers with his palm.

"Get a piece of cloth, boy. That is not the way to clean things. Get a piece of cloth, Swami," Father said, half kindly and half impatiently.

Swaminathan looked about and complained, "I can't find any here, Father."

"Run and see."

This was a welcome suggestion. Swaminathan hurried out. He first went to his grandmother.

"Granny, get me a piece of cloth, quick."

"Where am I to go for a piece of cloth?"

"Where am I to go?" he asked peevishly, and added quite irrelevantly, "If one has got to read even during holidays, I don't see why holidays are given at all."

"What is the matter?"

This was his opportunity to earn some sympathy. He almost wept as he said: "I don't know what Rajam and Mani will think, waiting for me there, if I keep on fooling here. Granny, if Father cannot find any work to do, why shouldn't he go and sleep?"

Father shouted across the hall: "Did you find the cloth?"

Swaminathan answered: "Granny hasn't got it. I shall see if Mother has." His mother was sitting in the back corridor on a mat, with the baby sleeping on her lap. Swaminathan glared at her. Her advice to her husband a few minutes ago rankled in his heart. "You are a fine lady, Mother," he said in an undertone, "why don't you leave us poor folk alone?"

"What?" she asked, unconscious of the sarcasm, and having forgotten what she had said to her husband a few minutes ago.

"You needn't have gone and carried tales against me. I don't know what I have done to you." He would have enjoyed prolonging this talk, but Father was waiting for the duster.

"Can you give me a piece of cloth?" he asked, coming to business.

"What cloth?"

"What cloth! How should I know? It seems I have got to tidy up those—those books of mine. A fine way of spending the holidays!"

"I can't get any now."

"H'm. You can't, can't you?" He looked about. There was a piece of cloth under the baby. In a flash, he stooped, rolled the baby over, pulled out the cloth, and was off. He held his mother responsible for all his troubles, and disturbing the baby and snatching its cloth gave him great relief.

With a fierce satisfaction he tilted the table and tipped all the things on it over the floor, and then picked them up one by one, and arranged them on the table.

Father watched him. "Is this how you arrange things? You have kept all the light things at the bottom and the heavy ones on top. Take out those notebooks. Keep the atlas at the bottom."

Mother came in with the baby in her arms and complained to Father, "Look at that boy, he has taken the baby's cloth. Is there nobody to control him, in this house? I wonder how long his school is going to be kept closed."

Swaminathan continued his work with concentrated interest. Father was pleased to ignore Mother's complaint; he merely pinched the sleeping baby's cheeks, at which Mother was annoyed and left the room.

Half an hour later Swaminathan sat in his father's room in a chair, with a slate in his hand and pencil ready. Father held the arithmetic book open and dictated: "'Rama has ten mangoes with which he wants to earn fifteen *annas*. Krishna wants only four mangoes. How much will Krishna have to pay?'"

Swaminathan gazed and gazed at this sum, and every time he read it, it seemed to acquire a new meaning. He had the feeling of having stepped into a fearful maze...

His mouth began to water at the thought of mangoes. He wondered what made Rama fix fifteen *annas* for ten mangoes. What kind of a man was Rama? Probably he was like Sankar. Somehow one couldn't help feeling that he must have been like Sankar, with his ten mangoes and his iron determination to get fifteen *annas*. If Rama was like Sankar, Krishna must have been like the Pea. Here Swaminathan felt an unaccountable sympathy for Krishna.

"Have you done the sum?" Father asked, looking over the newspaper he was reading.

"Father, will you tell me if the mangoes were ripe?"

Father regarded him for a while and smothering a smile remarked: "Do the sum first. I will tell you whether the fruits were ripe or not, afterwards."

Swaminathan felt utterly helpless. If only Father would tell him whether Rama was trying to sell ripe fruits or unripe ones! Of what avail would it be to tell him afterwards? He felt strongly that the answer to this question contained the key to the whole problem. It would be scandalous to expect fifteen *annas* for ten unripe mangoes. But even if he did, it wouldn't be unlike Rama, whom Swaminathan was steadily beginning to hate and invest with the darkest qualities.

"Father, I cannot do the sum," Swaminathan said pushing away the slate.

"What is the matter with you? You can't solve a simple problem in Simple Proportion?"

"We are not taught this kind of thing in our school."

"Get the slate here. I will make you give the answer now." Swaminathan waited with interest for the miracle to happen. Father studied the sum for a second and asked: "What is the price of ten mangoes?"

Swaminathan looked over the sum to find out which part of the sum contained an answer to this question. "I don't know."

"You seem to be an extraordinary idiot. Now read the sum. Come on. How much does Rama expect for ten mangoes?"

"Fifteen *annas* of course," Swaminathan thought, but how could that be its price, just price? It was very well for Rama to expect it in his avarice. But was it the right price? And then there was the obscure point whether the mangoes were ripe or not. If they were ripe, fifteen *annas* might not be an improbable price. If only he could get more light on this point!

"How much does Rama want for his mangoes?"

"Fifteen *annas*," replied Swaminathan without conviction.

"Very good. How many mangoes does Krishna want?"

"Four."

"What is the price of four?"

Father seemed to delight in torturing him. How could he know? How could he know what that fool Krishna would pay?

"Look here, boy. I have half a mind to thrash you. What have you in your head? Ten mangoes cost fifteen *annas*. What is the price of one? Come on. If you don't say it—"

His hand took Swaminathan's ear and gently twisted it. Swaminathan could not open his mouth because he could not decide whether the solution lay in the realm of addition, subtraction, multiplication, or division. The longer he hesitated, the more violent the twist was becoming. In the end when Father was waiting with a scowl for an answer, he received only a squeal from his son. "I am not going to leave you till you tell me how much a single mango costs at fifteen *annas* for ten."

What was the matter with Father? Swaminathan kept blinking. Where was the urgency to know its price? Anyway, if Father wanted so badly to know, instead of harassing him, let him go to the market and find it out. The whole brood of Ramas and Krishnas, with their endless transactions with odd quantities of mangoes and fractions of money, were getting disgusting.

Father admitted defeat by declaring: "One mango costs fifteen over ten *annas*. Simplify it."

Here he was being led to the most hideous regions of arithmetic—fractions. "Give me the slate, Father. I will find it out." He worked and found at the end of fifteen minutes: "The price of one mango is three over two *annas*."

He expected to be contradicted any moment. But Father said: "Very good, simplify it further."

It was plain sailing after that. Swaminathan announced at the end of half an hour's agony: "Krishna must pay six *annas*," and burst into tears.

***

At five o'clock when he was ready to start for the club, Swaminathan's father felt sorry for having worried his son all the afternoon. "Would you like to come with me to the club, boy?" he asked when he saw Swaminathan sulking behind a pillar with a woebegone face. Swaminathan answered by disappearing for a minute and reappearing dressed in his coat and cap. Father surveyed him from head to foot and remarked: "Why can't you be a little more tidy?" Swaminathan writhed awkwardly.

"Lakshmi," Father called, and said to Mother when she came: "There must be a clean dress for the boy in the box. Give him something clean."

"Please don't worry about it now," said Mother. "He is all right. Who is to open the box? The keys are somewhere...I have just mixed milk for the baby—"

"What has happened to all his dresses?"

"What dresses? You haven't bought a square inch of cloth since last summer."

"What do you mean? What has happened to all the pieces of twill I bought a few months ago?" he demanded vaguely, making a mental note at the same time, to take the boy to the tailor on Wednesday evening. Swaminathan was relieved to find his mother reluctant to get him a fresh dress, since he had an obscure dread that his father would leave him behind and go away if he went in to change.

A car hooted in front of the house. Father snatched his tennis racket from a table and rushed out followed by Swaminathan. A gentleman, wearing a blazer that appealed to Swaminathan, sat at the wheel, and said: "Good evening," with a grin. Swaminathan was at first afraid that this person might refuse to take him in the car. But his fears were dispelled by the gentleman's saying amiably: "Hallo, Srinivasan, are you bringing your boy to the club? Righto!" Swaminathan sat in the back seat while his father and his friend occupied the front.

The car whizzed along. Swaminathan was elated and wished that some of his friends could see him then. The car slid into a gate and came to a stop amidst half a dozen other cars.

He watched his father playing tennis, and came to the conclusion that he was the best player in all the three courts that were laid side by side. Swaminathan found that whenever his father hit the ball, his opponents were unable to receive it and so let it go and strike the screen. He also found that the picker's life was one of grave risks.

Swaminathan fell into a pleasant state of mind. The very fact that he was allowed to be present there and watch the play gave him a sense of importance. He would have something to say to his friends tomorrow. He slowly moved and stood near the screen behind his father. Before stationing himself there, he wondered for a moment if the little fellow in khaki dress might not object. But the little fellow was busy picking up balls and throwing them at the players. Swaminathan stayed there for about ten minutes. His father's actions were clearer to watch from behind, and the twang of his racket when hitting the ball was very pleasing to the ear.

For a change Swaminathan stood looking at the boy in khaki dress. As he gazed, his expression changed. He blinked fast as if he disbelieved his eyes. It was the coachman's son, only slightly transformed by the khaki dress! Now the boy had turned and seen him. He grinned maliciously and hastily took out of his pocket a penknife, and held it up. Swaminathan was seized with cold fear. He moved away fast unobtrusively, to his former place, which was at a safe distance from his enemy.

After the set when his father walked towards the building, Swaminathan took care to walk a little in front of him and not behind, as he feared that he might get a stab any minute in his back.

"Swami, don't go in front. You are getting under my feet." Swaminathan obeyed with a reluctant heart. He kept shooting glances sideways and behind. He stooped and picked up a stone, a sharp stone, and held it ready for use if any emergency should arise. The distance from the tennis court to the building was about a dozen yards, but to Swaminathan it seemed to be a mile and a half.

He felt safe when he sat in a chair beside his father in the card-room. A thick cloud of smoke floated in the air. Father was shuffling and throwing cards with great zest. This was the safest place on earth. There was Father and any number of his friends, and let the coachman's son try a hand if he liked. A little later Swaminathan looked out of the window and felt disturbed at the sight of the stars. It would be darker still by the time the card game finished and Father rose to go home.

An hour later Father rose from the table. Swaminathan was in a highly nervous state when he got down the last steps of the building. There were unknown dangers lurking in the darkness around. He was no doubt secure between Father and his friend. That thought was encouraging. But Swaminathan felt at the same time that it would have been better if all the persons in the card-room had escorted him to the car. He needed all the guarding he could get, and some more. Probably by this time the boy had gone out and brought a huge gang of assassins and was waiting for him. He could not walk in front as, in addition to getting under his father's feet, he had no idea which way they had to go for the car. Following his father was out of the question, as he might not reach the car at all. He walked in a peculiar side-step which enabled him to see before him and behind him simultaneously. The distance was interminable. He decided to explain the danger to Father and seek his protection.

"Father."

"Well, boy?"

Swaminathan suddenly decided that his father had better not know anything about the coachman's son, however serious the situation might be.

"What do you want, boy?" Father asked again.

"Father, are we going home now?"

"Yes."

"Walking?"

"No. The car is there, near the gate."

When they came to the car, Swaminathan got in first and occupied the centre of the back seat. He was still in suspense. Father's friend was taking time to start the car. Swaminathan was sitting all alone in the back seat, very far behind Father and his friend. Even now, the coachman's son and his gang could easily pull him out and finish him.

The car started. When its engine rumbled, it sounded to Swaminathan's ears like the voice of a saviour. The car was outside the gate now and picked up speed. Swaminathan lifted a corner of his *dhoti* and mopped his brow.

12

BROKEN PANES

On the 15th of August 1930, about two thousand citizens of Malgudi assembled on the right bank of Sarayu to protest against the arrest of Gauri Sankar, a prominent political worker of Bombay. An earnest-looking man clad in *khaddar* stood on a wooden platform and addressed the gathering. In a high, piercing voice, he sketched the life and achievements of Gauri Sankar; and after that passed on to generalities: "We are slaves today," he shrieked, "worse slaves than we have ever been before. Let us remember our heritage. Have we forgotten the glorious periods of *Ramayana* and *Mahabharata*? This is the country that has given the world a *Kalidasa*, a *Buddha*, a *Sankara*. Our ships sailed the high seas and we had reached the height of civilization when the Englishman ate raw flesh and wandered in the jungles, nude. But now what are we?" He paused and said on the inspiration of the moment, without troubling to verify the meaning: "We are slaves of slaves." To Swaminathan, as to Mani, this part of the speech was incomprehensible. But five minutes later the speaker said something that seemed practicable: "Just think for a while. We are three hundred and thirty-six millions, and our land is as big as Europe minus Russia. England is no bigger than our Madras Presidency and is inhabited by a handful of white rogues and is thousands of miles away. Yet we bow in homage before the Englishman! Why are we become, through no fault of our own, docile and timid? It is the bureaucracy that has made us so, by intimidation and starvation. You need not do more. Let every Indian spit on England, and the quantity of saliva will be enough to drown England..."

"Gandhi ki Jai," shouted Swaminathan involuntarily, deeply stirred by the speaker's eloquence at this point. He received a fierce dig from Mani, who whispered: "Fool! Why can't you hold your tongue?"

Swaminathan asked: "Is it true?"

"Which?"

"Spitting and drowning the Europeans."

"Must be, otherwise do you think that fellow would suggest it?"

"Then why not do it? It is easy."

"Europeans will shoot us, they have no heart," said Mani. This seemed a satisfactory answer, and Swaminathan was about to clear up another doubt when one or two persons sitting around frowned at him.

For the rest of the evening Swaminathan was caught in the lecturer's eloquence; so was Mani. With the lecturer they wept over the plight of the Indian peasant; resolved to boycott English goods, especially Lancashire and Manchester cloth, as the owners of those mills had cut off the thumbs of the weavers of Dacca muslin, for which India was famous at one time. What muslin it was, a whole piece of forty yards could be folded and kept in a snuff box! The persons who cut off the thumbs of such weavers deserved the worst punishment possible. And Swaminathan was going to mete it out by wearing only *khaddar*, the rough homespun. He looked at the dress he was just then wearing, in chagrin. "Mani," he said in a low voice, "have you any idea what I am wearing?"

Mani examined Swaminathan's coat and declared: "It is Lancashire cloth."

"How do you know it?"

Mani glared at him in answer.

"What are you wearing?" asked Swaminathan.

"Of course *khaddar*. Do you think I will pay a paisa to those Lancashire devils? No. They won't get it out of me."

Swaminathan had his own doubts over this statement. But he preferred to keep quiet, and wished that he had come out nude rather than in what he believed to be Lancashire cloth.

A great cry burst from the crowd: *"Bharat Matha ki Jai!"* And then there were cries of *"Gandhi ki Jai!"* After that came a kind of mournful 'national' song. The evening's programme closed with a bonfire of foreign cloth. It was already dark. Suddenly the darkness was lit up by a red glare. A fire was lighted. A couple of boys wearing Gandhi caps went round begging people to burn their foreign cloth. Coats and caps and upper cloth came whizzing through the air and fell with a thud into the fire, which purred and crackled and rose high, thickening the air with smoke and a burnt smell. People moved about like dim shadows in the red glare. Swaminathan was watching the scene with little shivers of joy going down his spine. Somebody asked him: "Young man, do you want our country to remain in eternal slavery?"

"No, no," Swaminathan replied.

"But you are wearing a foreign cap."

Swaminathan quailed with shame. "Oh, I didn't notice," he said, and removing his cap flung it into the fire with a feeling that he was saving the country.

***

Early next morning as Swaminathan lay in bed watching a dusty beam of sunlight falling a few yards off his bed, his mind, which was just emerging from sleep, became conscious of a vague worry. Swaminathan asked himself what that worry was. It must be something connected with school. Homework? No. Matters were all right in that direction. It was something connected with dress. Bonfire, bonfire of clothes. Yes. It now dawned upon him with an oppressive clearness that he had thrown his cap into the patriotic bonfire of the previous evening; and of course his father knew nothing about it.

What was he going to wear for school today? Telling his father and asking for a new cap was not practicable. He could not go to school bareheaded.

He started for the school in a mood of fatalistic abandon, with only a coat and no cap on. And the fates were certainly kind to him. At least Swaminathan believed that he saw the hand of God in it when he reached the school and found the boys gathered in the road in front of the school in a noisy irregular mob.

Swaminathan passed through the crowd unnoticed till he reached the school gate. A perfect stranger belonging to the Third Form stopped him and asked: "Where are you going?" Swaminathan hesitated for a moment to discover if there was any trap in this question and said: "Why—er...Of course..."

"No school today," declared the stranger with emphasis, and added passionately, "one of the greatest sons of the motherland has been sent to gaol."

"I won't go to school," Swaminathan said, greatly relieved at this unexpected solution to his cap problem.

The headmaster and the teachers were standing in the front veranda of the school. The headmaster looked care-worn. Ebenezar was swinging his cane and pacing up and down. For once, the boys saw D. Pillai, the history teacher, serious, and gnawing his close-clipped moustache in great agitation. The crowd in the road had become brisker and noisier, and the school looked forlorn. At five minutes to ten the first bell rang, hardly heard by anyone except those standing near the gate. A conference was going on between the teachers and the headmaster. The headmaster's hand trembled as he pulled out his watch and gave orders for the second bell. The bell that at other times gave out a clear rich note now sounded weak and inarticulate. The headmaster and the teacher were seen coming toward the gate, and a lull came upon the mob.

The headmaster appealed to the boys to behave and get back to their classes quietly. The boys stood firm. The teachers, including D. Pillai, tried and failed. After uttering a warning that the punishment to follow would be severe, the headmaster withdrew. Thundering shouts of *"Bharat Matha ki Jai!"* *"Gandhi ki Jai!"* and *"Gauri Sankar ki Jai!"* followed him.

There were gradual unnoticed additions of all sorts of people to the original student mob. Now zestful adult voices could be detected in the frequent cries of *"Gandhi ki Jai!"*

Half a dozen persons appointed themselves leaders, and ran about crying: "Remember, this is a *hartal*. This is a day of mourning. Observe it in the proper spirit of sorrow and silence."

Swaminathan was an unobserved atom in the crowd. Another unobserved atom was busily piling up small stones before him, and dinging them with admirable aim at the panes in the front part of the school building. Swaminathan could hardly help following his example. He picked up a handful of stones and searched the building with his eyes. He was disappointed to find at least seventy per cent of the panes already attended to.

He uttered a sharp cry of joy as he discovered a whole ventilator, consisting of small square glasses, in the headmaster's room, intact! He sent a stone at it and waited with cocked-up ears for the splintering noise as the stone hit the glass, and the final shivering noise, a fraction of a second later, as the piece crashed on the floor. It was thrilling.

A puny man came running into the crowd announcing excitedly, "Work is going on in the Board High School."

This horrible piece of news set the crowd in motion. A movement began towards the Board High School, which was situated at the tail-end of Market Road.

When they reached the Board High School, the self-appointed leaders held up their hands, requested the crowd to remain outside and be peaceful, and entered the school themselves. Within fifteen minutes, trickling in by twos and threes, the crowd was in the school hall.

A spokesman of the crowd said to the headmaster, "Sir, we are not here to create a disturbance. We only want you to close the school. It is imperative. Our leader is in gaol. Our motherland is in the throes of war."

The headmaster, a wizened owl-like man, screamed, "With whose permission did you enter the building? Kindly go out. Or I shall send for the police."

This was received with howling, jeering, and hooting. And following it, tables and benches were overturned and broken, and window-panes were smashed. Most of the Board School boys merged with the crowd. A few, however, stood apart. They were first invited to come out; but when they showed reluctance, they were dragged out.

Swaminathan's part in all this was by no means negligible. It was he who shouted "We will spit on the police" (though it was drowned in the din), when the headmaster mentioned the police. The mention of the police had sent his blood boiling. What brazenness, what shamelessness, to talk of police—the nefarious agents of the Lancashire thumb-cutters! When the pandemonium started, he was behind no one in destroying the school furniture. With tremendous joy he discovered that there were many glass panes untouched yet. His craving to break them could not be fully satisfied in his own school. He ran round collecting ink-bottles and flung them one by one at every pane that caught his eye. When the Board School boys were dragged out, he felt that he could not do much in that line, most of the boys being as big as himself. On the flash of a bright idea, he wriggled through the crowd and looked for the Infant Standards. There he found little children huddled together and shivering with fright. He charged into this crowd with such ferocity that the children scattered about, stumbling and falling. One unfortunate child who shuffled and moved awkwardly received individual attention. Swaminathan pounced upon him, pulled out his cap, threw it down and stamped on it, swearing at him all the time. He pushed him and dragged him this way and that and then gave him a blow on the head and left him to his fate.

Having successfully paralysed work in the Board School, the crowd moved on in a procession along Market Road. The air vibrated with the songs and slogans uttered in a hundred keys by a hundred voices. Swaminathan found himself wedged in among a lot of unknown people, in one of the last ranks. The glare from the blanched treeless Market Road was blinding. The white dust stirred up by the procession hung like thin mist in the air and choked him. He could see before him nothing but moving backs and shoulders and occasionally odd parts of some building. His throat was dry with shouting, and he was beginning to feel hungry. He was pondering whether he could just slip out and go home, when the procession came to a sudden halt. In a minute the rear ranks surged forward to see what the matter was.

The crowd was now in the centre of Market Road, before the fountain in the square. On the other side of the fountain were drawn up about fifty constables armed with *lathis*. About a dozen of them held up the procession. A big man, with a cane in his hand and a revolver slung from his belt, advanced towards the procession. His leather straps and belts and the highly-polished boots and hose made him imposing in Swaminathan's eyes. When he turned his head Swaminathan saw to his horror that it was Rajam's father! Swaminathan could not help feeling sorry that it should be Rajam's father. Rajam's father! Rajam's father to be at the head of those traitors!

The Deputy Superintendent of Police fixed his eyes on his wrist-watch and said, "I declare this assembly unlawful. I give it five minutes to disperse." At the end of five minutes he looked up and uttered in a hollow voice the word, "Charge."

In the confusion that followed Swaminathan was very nearly trampled upon and killed. The policemen rushed into the crowd, pushing and beating everybody. Swaminathan had joined a small group of panic-stricken runners. The policemen came towards them with upraised *lathis*. Swaminathan shrieked to them, "Don't kill me. I know nothing." He then heard a series of dull noises as the *lathis* descended on the bodies of his neighbours. Swaminathan saw blood streaming from the forehead of one. Down came the *lathis* again. Another runner fell down with a groan. On the back of a third the *lathis* fell again and again.

Swaminathan felt giddy with fear. He was running as fast as his legs could carry him. But the policemen kept pace with him; one of them held him up by his hair and asked, "What business have you here?"

"I don't know anything, leave me, sirs," Swaminathan pleaded.

"Doing nothing! Mischievous monkey!" said the grim, hideous policeman—how hideous policemen were at close quarters!—and delivering him a light tap on the head with the *lathi,* ordered him to run before he was kicked.

***

Swaminathan's original intention had been to avoid that day's topic before his father. But as soon as Father came home, even before taking off his coat, he called Mother and gave her a summary of the day's events. He spoke with a good deal of warmth. "The Deputy Superintendent is a butcher," he said as he went in to change. Swaminathan was disposed to agree that the Deputy Superintendent was a butcher, as he recollected the picture of Rajam's father looking at his watch, grimly ticking off seconds before giving orders for massacre.

Father came out of the dressing-room before undoing his tie, to declare: "Fifty persons have been taken to the hospital with dangerous contusions. One or two are also believed to be killed." Turning to Swaminathan he said, "I heard that schoolboys have given a lot of trouble, what did you do?"

"There was a strike…" replied Swaminathan and discovered here an opportunity to get his cap problem solved. He added, "Oh, the confusion! You know, somebody pulled off the cap that I was wearing and tore it to bits…I want a cap before I start for school tomorrow."

"Who was he?" Father asked.

"I don't know, some bully in the crowd."

"Why did he do it?"

"Because it was foreign . . ."

"Who said so? I paid two rupees and got it from the Khaddar Stores. It is a black *khaddar* cap. Why do you presume that you know what is what?"

"I didn't do anything. I was very nearly assaulted when I resisted."

"You should have knocked him down. I bought the cap and the cloth for your coat on the same day in the Khaddar Stores. If any man says that they are not *khaddar*, he must be blind."

"People say that it was made in Lancashire."

"Nonsense. You can ask them to mind their business. And if you allow your clothes to be torn by people who think this and that, you will have to go about naked, that is all. And you may also tell them that I won't have a paisa of mine sent to foreign countries. I know my duty. Whatever it is, why do not you urchins leave politics alone and mind your business? We have enough troubles in our country without you brats messing up things . . ."

Swaminathan lay wide awake in bed for a long time. As the hours advanced, and one by one as the lights in the house disappeared, his body compelled him to take stock of the various injuries done to it during the day. His elbows and knees had their own tales to tell: they brought back to his mind the three or four falls that he had had that day. One was—when?—yes, when Rajam got down from his car and came to the school, and Swaminathan had wanted to hide himself, and in the hurry stumbled on a heap of stones, and there the knees were badly skinned. And again when the policemen charged, he ran and fell flat before a shop, and some monster ran over him, pinning him with one foot to the ground.

Now as he turned there was a pang about his hips. And then he felt as if a load had been hung from his thighs. And again as he thought of it, he felt a heavy monotonous pain in the head—the merciless rascals! The policeman's *lathi* was none too gentle. And he had been called a monkey! He would—he would see—to call him a monkey! He was no monkey. Only they—the policemen—looked like monkeys, and they behaved like monkeys too.

***

The headmaster entered the class with a slightly flushed face and a hard ominous look in his eyes. Swaminathan wished that he had been anywhere but there at that moment. The headmaster surveyed the class for a few minutes and asked, "Are you not ashamed to come and sit there after what you did yesterday?" Just as a special honour to them, he read out the names of a dozen or so that had attended the class. After that he read out the names of those that had kept away, and asked them to stand on their benches. He felt that that punishment was not enough and asked them to stand on their desks. Swaminathan was among them and felt humiliated at that eminence.

Then they were lectured. When it was over, they were asked to offer explanations one by one. One said that he had had an attack of headache and therefore could not come to the school. He was asked to bring a medical certificate. The second said that while he had been coming to the school on the previous day, someone had told him that there would be no school, and he had gone back home. The headmaster replied that if he was going to listen to every loafer who said there would be no school, he deserved to be flogged. Anyway, why did he not come to the school and verify? No answer. The punishment was pronounced: ten days' attendance cancelled, two rupees fine, and the whole day to be spent on the desk. The third said that he had had an attack of headache. The fourth said that he had had stomach-ache. The fifth said that his grandmother died suddenly just as he was starting for the school. The headmaster asked him if he could bring a letter from his father. No. He had no father. Then, who was his guardian? His grandmother. But the grandmother was dead, was she not? No. It was another grandmother. The headmaster asked how many grandmothers a person could have. No answer. Could he bring a letter from his neighbours? No, he could not. None of his neighbours could read or write, because he lived in one of the more illiterate parts of Ellaman Street. Then the headmaster offered to send a teacher to this illiterate locality to ascertain from the boy's neighbours if the death of the grandmother was a fact. A pause, some perspiration and then the answer that the neighbours could not possibly know anything about it, since the grandmother died in the village. The headmaster hit him on the knuckles with his cane, called him a street dog, and pronounced the punishment: fifteen days' suspension.

When Swaminathan's turn came, he looked around helplessly. Rajam sat on the third bench in front, and resolutely looked away. He was gazing at the blackboard intently. But yet the back of his head and the pink ears were visible to Swaminathan. It was an intolerable sight. Swaminathan was in acute suspense lest that head should turn and fix its eyes on his; he felt that he would drop from the desk to the floor, if that happened. The pink ears three benches off made him incapable of speech. If only somebody would put a blackboard between his eyes and those pink ears!

He was deaf to the question that the headmaster was putting to him. A rap on his body from the headmaster's cane brought him to himself.

"Why did you keep away yesterday?" asked the headmaster, looking up.

Swaminathan's first impulse was to protest that he had never been absent. But the attendance register was there. "No—no—I was stoned. I tried to come, but they took away my cap and burnt it. Many strong men held me down when I tried to come...When a great man is sent to gaol...I am surprised to see you a slave of the Englishmen...Didn't they cut off—Dacca muslin—slaves of slaves..." These were some of the disjointed explanations which streamed into his head, and which, even at that moment, he was discreet enough not to express. He had wanted to mention a headache, but he found to his distress that others beside him had had one.

The headmaster shouted, "Won't you open your mouth?" He brought the cane sharply down on Swaminathan's right shoulder. Swaminathan kept staring at the headmaster with tearful eyes, massaging with his left hand the spot where the cane was laid. "I will kill you if you keep on staring without answering my question," cried the headmaster.

"I—I—couldn't come," stammered Swaminathan.

"Is that so?" asked the headmaster, and turning to a boy said, "Bring the peon."

Swaminathan thought: "What, is he going to ask the peon to thrash me? If he does any such thing, I will bite everybody dead." The peon came. The headmaster said to him, "Now say what you know about this rascal on the desk."

The peon eyed Swaminathan with a sinister look, grunted and demanded, "Didn't I see you break the panes...?"

"Of the ventilators in my room?" added the headmaster with zest.

Here there was no chance of escape. Swaminathan kept staring foolishly till he received another whack on the back. The headmaster demanded what the young brigand had to say about it. The brigand had nothing to say. It was a fact that he had broken the panes. They had seen it. There was nothing more to it. He had unconsciously become defiant and did not care to deny the charge. When another whack came on his back, he ejaculated, "Don't beat me, sir. It pains."

This was an invitation to the headmaster to bring down the cane four times again. He said, "Keep standing here, on this desk, staring like an idiot, till I announce your dismissal."

Every pore in Swaminathan's body burnt with the touch of the cane. He had a sudden flood of courage, the courage that comes of desperation. He restrained the tears that were threatening to rush out, jumped down, and, grasping his books, rushed out muttering, "I don't care for your dirty school."

13
THE 'M.C.C.'

Six weeks later Rajam came to Swaminathan's house to announce that he forgave him all his sins—starting with his political activities, to his new acquisition, the Board High School air—by which was meant a certain slowness and stupidity engendered by mental decay.

After making his exit from Albert Mission School in that theatrical manner on the day following the strike, Swaminathan became so consistently stubborn that a few days later his father took him to the Board School and admitted him there. At first Swaminathan was rather uncertain of his happiness in the new school. But he excited the curiosity that all newcomers do, and found himself to his great satisfaction the centre of attraction in Second C. All his new class-mates, remarkably new faces, often clustered round him to see him and hear him talk. He had not yet picked the few that he would have liked to call his chums. He still believed that his Albert Mission set was intact, though since the reopening in June the set was not what it had been before. Sankar disappeared, and people said that his father had been transferred; Somu was not promoted, and that meant he was automatically excluded from the group, the law being inexorable in that respect; the Pea was promoted, but he returned to the class exactly three months late, and he was quite full up with medical certificates, explanations, and exemptions. He was a man of a hundred worries now, and passed his old friends like a stranger. Only Rajam and Mani were still intact as far as Swaminathan was concerned. Mani saw him every day. But Rajam had not spoken to him since the day when his political doings became known.

And now this afternoon Swaminathan was sitting in a dark corner of the house trying to make a camera with a cardboard box and a spectacle lens. In his effort to fix the lens in the hole that was one round too large, he was on the point of losing his temper, when he heard a familiar voice calling him. He ran to the door.

"Hallo! Hallo! Rajam," he cried, "why didn't you tell me you were coming?"

"What is the thing in your hand?" Rajam asked.

"Oh," Swaminathan said, blushing.

"Come, come, let us have a look at it."

"Oh, it is nothing," Swaminathan said, giving him the box.

As Rajam kept gazing at the world through the hole in the cardboard box, Swaminathan said, "Akbar Ali of our class has made a marvellous camera."

"Has he? What does he do with it?"

"He has taken a lot of photos with it."

"Indeed! Photos of what?"

"He hasn't yet shown them to me, but they are probably photos of houses, people, and trees."

Rajam sat down on the doorstep and asked, "And who is this Akbar Ali?"

"He is a nice Muhammadan, belongs to our class."

"In the Board High School?" There was just a suspicion of a sneer in his tone.

Swaminathan preferred to ignore this question and continued, "He has a bicycle. He is a very fine Muhammadan, calls Muhammad of Gazni and Aurangazeb rascals."

"What makes you think that they were that?"

"Didn't they destroy our temples and torture the Hindus? Have you forgotten the Somnathpur God?"

"We *brahmins* deserve that and more," said Rajam. "In our house my father does not care for New-Moon days and there are no annual ceremonies for the dead." He was in a debating mood, and Swaminathan realized it and remained silent. Rajam said, "I tell you what, it is your Board High School that has given you this mentality."

Swaminathan felt that the safest course would be to agree with him. "You are right in a way. I don't like the Board High School."

"Then why did you go and join it?"

"I could not help it. You saw how beastly our master was. If you had been in my place, you would have kicked him in the face."

This piece of flattery did not soothe Rajam. "If I were you I would have kept clear of all your dirty politics and strikes." His father was a government servant, and hence his family was anti-political.

Swaminathan said, "You are right. I should have remained at home on the day of the strike."

This example of absolute submissiveness touched Rajam. He said promptly that he was prepared to forgive Swaminathan his past sins and would not mind his belonging to the Board School. They were to be friends as of old. "What would you say to a cricket team?" Rajam asked.

Swaminathan had not thought of cricket as something that he himself could play. He was, of course, familiar with Hobbs, Bradman, and Duleep, and vainly tried to carry their scores in his head, as Rajam did. He filched pictures of cricket players, as Rajam did, and pasted them in an album, though he secretly did not very much care for those pictures— there was something monotonous about them. He sometimes thought that the same picture was pasted in every page of the album.

"No, Rajam, I don't think I can play. I don't know how to play."

"That is what everybody thinks," said Rajam. "I don't know myself, though I collect pictures and scores."

This was very pleasing to hear. Probably Hobbs too was shy and sceptical before he took the bat and swung it.

"We can challenge a lot of teams, including our school eleven. They think they can't be beaten," said Swaminathan.

"What! The Board School mugs think that! We shall thrash them. Oh, yes."

"What shall we call it?"

"Don't you know? It is the M.C.C.," said Rajam.

"That is Hobbs's team, isn't it? They may drag us before a court if we take their name."

"Who says that? If we get into any trouble, I shall declare before the judge that M.C.C. stands for Malgudi Cricket Club."

Swaminathan was a little disappointed. Though as M.C.C. it sounded imposing, the name was really a bit tame. "I think we had better try some other name, Rajam."

"What would you suggest?"

"Well—I am for 'Friends Eleven'."

"Friends Eleven?"

"Or, say, 'Jumping Stars'?" said Swaminathan.

"Oh, that is not bad, not bad, you know."

"I do think it would be glorious to call ourselves 'Jumping Stars'!"

Rajam instantly had a vision of a newspaper report: "The Jumping Stars soundly thrashed the Board High School Eleven." "It is a beauty, I think," he cried, moved by the vision. He pulled out a piece of paper and a pencil, and said, "Come on, Swami, repeat the names that come to your head. It would be better to have a long list to select from. We shall underline 'Jumping Stars' and 'M.C.C.' and give them special consideration. Come on."

Swaminathan remained thoughtful and started, "'Friends Eleven'...'Jumping Stars'...'Friends Union'..."

"I have 'Friends Union' already here," Rajam said pointing to the list.

Swaminathan went on: "'Excelsiors'..."

"I have got it."

"'Excelsior Union'...'Champion Eleven'..." A long pause.

"Are you dried up?" Rajam asked.

"No, if Mani were here, he would have suggested a few more names...'Champion Eleven'."

"You have just said it."

"'Victory Union Eleven'..."

"That is very good. I think it is very very good. People would be afraid of us." He held the list before him and read the names with great satisfaction. He had struggled hard on the previous night to get a few names. But only 'Friends Union' and 'Excelsiors' kept coming till he felt fatigued. But what a lot of names Swaminathan was able to reel off. "Can you meet me tomorrow evening, Swami? I shall get Mani down. Let us select a name."

After a while Swaminathan asked, "Look here, do you think we shall have to pay tax or something to the Government when we start the team?"

"The Government seems to tax everything in this world. My father's pay is about five hundred. But nearly two hundred and over is demanded by the Government. Anyway, what makes you think that we shall have to pay tax?"

"I mean—if we don't pay tax, the Government may not recognize our team or its name and a hundred other teams may take the same name. It might lead to all sorts of complications."

"Suppose we have two names?" asked Rajam.

"It is not done."

"I know a lot of teams that have two names. When I was in Bishop Waller's, we had a cricket team that we called—I don't remember the name now. I think we called it 'Cricket Eleven' and 'Waller's Cricket Eleven'. You see, one name is for ordinary use and the other is for matches."

"It is all very well for a rich team like your Waller's. But suppose the Government demands two taxes from us?"

Rajam realized at this point that the starting of a cricket team was the most complicated problem on earth. He had simply expected to gather a dozen fellows on the *maidan* next to his compound and play, and challenge the world. But here were endless troubles, starting with the name that must be unique, Government taxes, and so on. The Government did not seem to know where it ought to interfere and where not. He had a momentary sympathy for Gandhi; no wonder he was dead against the Government.

Swaminathan seemed to be an expert in thinking out difficulties. He said, "Even if we want to pay, whom are we to pay the taxes to?" Certainly not to His Majesty or the Viceroy. Who was the Government? What if somebody should take the money and defraud them, somebody pretending to be the Government? Probably they would have to send the taxes by Money Order to the Governor! Well, that might be treason. And then what was the amount to be paid?

***

They sat round Rajam's table in his room. Mani held before him a catalogue of Messrs Binns, the Shop for Sports Goods. He read, "'Junior Willard Bats, Seven Eight, made of finest seasoned wood, used by Cambridge Junior Boys' Eleven'."

"Let me have a look at it..." said Rajam. He bent over the table and said, "Seems to be a fine bat. Have a look at it, Swami."

Swaminathan craned his neck and agreed that it was a fine bat, but he was indiscreet enough to say, "It looks like any other bat in the catalogue."

Mani's left hand shot out and held his neck and pressed his face close to the picture of the bat: "Why do you pretend to be a cricket player if you cannot see the difference between Junior Willard and other bats? You are not fit to be even a sweeper in our team." After this admonition the hold was relaxed.

Rajam asked, "Swami, do you know what the catalogue man calls the Junior Willard? It seems it is the Rolls-Royce among the junior bats. Don't you know the difference between the Rolls-Royce and other cars?"

Swaminathan replied haughtily, "I never said I saw no difference between the Rolls-Royce and other cars."

"What is the difference?" urged Rajam.

Mani laughed and teased, "Come on. If you really know the difference, why don't you say it?"

Swaminathan said, "The Rolls costs a lakh of rupees, while other cars cost about ten thousand; a Rolls has engines made of silver, while other cars have iron engines."

"Oh, oh!" jeered Rajam.

"A Rolls never gives trouble, while other cars always give trouble; a Rolls engine never stops; a Rolls-Royce never makes a noise, while other cars always make a noise."

"Why not deliver a lecture on the Rolls-Royce?" asked Mani.

"Swami, I am glad you know so much about the Rolls-Royce. I am at the same time ashamed to find you knowing so little about Willard Junior. We had about a dozen Willard Juniors when I was in Bishop Waller's. Oh! what bats! There are actual springs inside the bat, so that when you touch the ball it flies. There is fine silk cord wound round the handle. You don't know anything, and yet you talk! Show me another bat which has silk cord and springs like the Willard."

There was a pause, and after that Rajam said, "Note it down, Swami." Swaminathan noted down on a paper, 'Vilord june-ear bat.' And looking up asked, "How many?"

"Say three. Will that do, Mani?"

"Why waste money on three bats? Two will do..."

"But suppose one breaks in the middle of a match?" Rajam asked.

"Do you suppose we are going to supply bats to our opponents? They will have to come provided with bats. We must make it clear."

"Even then, if our bat breaks we may have to stop playing."

"Two will do, Rajam, unless you want to waste money."

Rajam's enthusiasm was great. He left his chair and sat on the arm of Mani's chair, gloating over the pictures of cricket goods in the catalogue, Swaminathan, though he was considered to be a bit of a heretic, caught the enthusiasm and perched on the other arm of the chair. All the three devoured with their eyes the glossy pictures of cricket balls, bats, and nets.

In about an hour they selected from the catalogue their team's requirements. And then came the most

135

difficult part of the whole affair—a letter to Messrs Binns, ordering goods. Bare courtesy made Rajam offer the authorship of the letter to Mani, who declined it. Swaminathan was forced to accept it in spite of his protests, and he sat for a long time chewing his pencil without producing a word; he had infinite trouble with spelling, and the more he tried to be correct the more muddled he was becoming; in the end he sat so long thinking of spelling that even such words as 'the' and 'and' became doubtful. Rajam took up the task himself. Half an hour later he placed on the table a letter:

From

M.C.C. (And Victory Union Eleven), Malgudi.

To

Messrs Binns,

Sportsmen,

Mount Road,

Madras.

DEAR SIR,

Please send to our team two junior willard bats, six balls, wickets and other things quick. It is very urgent. We shall send you money afterwards. Don't fear. Please be urgent.

Yours obediently,

CAPTAIN RAJAM (Captain).

This letter received Swaminathan's benedictions. But Mani expressed certain doubts. He wanted to know whether 'Dear' could stand at the beginning of a letter to a perfect stranger. "How can you call Binns 'Dear Sir'? You must say 'Sir'."

Rajam's explanation was: "I won't say 'Sir'. It is said only by clerks. I am not Binns's clerk. I don't care to address him as 'Sir'."

So this letter went as it was.

After this exacting work they were resting, with a feeling of relief, when the postman came in with a card for Rajam. Rajam read it and cried, "Guess who has written this?"

"Binns."

"Silly. It must be our headmaster."

"Somebody."

"J. B. Hobbs."

"It is from Sankar," Rajam announced joyfully.

"Sankar! We had almost forgotten that old thief." Swaminathan and Mani tore the card from Rajam's hand and read:

MY DEAR FRIEND,

I am studying here because my father came here. My mother is also here. All of us are here. And we will be only here. I am doing well. I hope you are doing well. It is very hot here. I had fever for three days and drank medicine. I hope I will read well and pass the examination. Is Swami and Mani doing well! It is very hot here. I am playing cricket now. I can't write more.

With regards,

your dearest friend,

SANKAR.

P. S. Don't forget me.

S.

They were profoundly moved by this letter, and decided to reply at once.

Three letters were ready in an hour. Mani copied Sankar's letter verbatim. Swaminathan and Rajam wrote nearly similar letters: they said they were doing well by the grace of God; they hoped that Sankar would pass and also that he was doing well; then they said a lot about their cricket team and hoped that Sankar would become a member; they also said that Sankar's team might challenge them to a match.

The letters were put into a stamped envelope, and the flap was pasted. It was only then that they felt the need of knowing Sankar's address. They searched all parts of Sankar's card. Not a word anywhere, not even the name of the town he was writing from. They tried to get this out of the postmark. But a dark curved smudge on the stamp cannot be very illuminating.

***

The M.C.C. and its organizers had solid proof that they were persons of count when a letter from Binns came addressed to the Captain, M.C.C., Malgudi. It was a joy, touching that beautiful envelope and turning it over in the hand. Binns were the first to recognize the M.C.C., and Rajam took a vow that he would buy every bit that his team needed from that great firm. There were three implications in this letter that filled Rajam and his friends with rapture: *(1)* that His Majesty's Post Office recognized their team was proved by the fact that the letter addressed to the captain was promptly delivered to him; *(2)* that they were really recognized by such a magnificent firm as Binns of Madras was proved by the fact that Binns cared to reply in a full letter and not on a card, and actually typed the letter! *(3)* Binns sent under another cover carrying four *annas* postage a huge catalogue. What a tribute!

The letter informed the captain that Messrs Binns thanked him for his letter and would be much obliged to him if he would kindly remit 25 per cent with the order and the balance could be paid against the V.P.P. of the railway receipt.

Three heads buzzed over the meaning of this letter. The trouble was that they could not understand whether Binns were going to send the goods or not. Mani promised to unravel the letter if somebody would tell him what 'obliged' meant. When they turned the pages of a dictionary and offered him the meaning, he was none the wiser. He felt that it was a meaningless word in that place.

"One thing is clear," said Rajam, "Binns thanks us for our letter. So I don't think this letter could mean a refusal to supply us goods."

Swaminathan agreed with him, "That is right. If he did not wish to supply you with things, would he thank you? He would have abused you." He scrutinized the letter again to make sure that there was no mistake about the thanks.

"Why has the fool used this word?" Mani asked, referring to 'obliged' which he could not pronounce. "It has no meaning. Is he trying to make fun of us?"

"He says something about twenty-five per cent. I wish I knew what it was," said Rajam.

Swaminathan could hardly contain himself, "I say, Rajam, I am surprised that you cannot understand this letter; you got sixty per cent in the last examination."

"Have you any sense in you? What has that to do with this? Even a B.A. cannot understand this letter."

In the end they came to the conclusion that the letter was sent to them by mistake. As far as they could see, the M.C.C. had written nothing in their previous letter to warrant such expressions as 'obliged', 'remit', and '25 per cent'. It could not be that the great firm of Binns were trying to make fun of them. Swaminathan pointed out 'To the Captain, M.C.C.' at the beginning of the letter. But he was told that it was also a part of the mistake.

This letter was put in a cover with a covering letter and dispatched. The covering letter said:

We are very sorry that you sent me somebody's letter. We are returning this somebody's letter. Please send our things immediately.

The M.C.C. were an optimistic lot. Though they were still unhonoured with a reply to their second letter, they expected the goods to arrive with every post. After ten days they thought they would start playing with whatever was available till they got the real bats, et cetera. The bottom of a dealwood case provided them with three good bats, and Rajam managed to get three used tennis balls from his father's club. The Pea was there, offering four real stumps that he believed he had somewhere in his house. A neat slip of ground adjoining Rajam's bungalow was to be the pitch. Everything was ready. Even if Binns took a month more to manufacture the goods specially for the M.C.C. (as they faintly thought probable), there need be no delay in starting practice. By the time the real bats and the balls arrived, they would be in form to play matches.

Rajam had chosen from his class a few who, he thought, deserved to become members of the M.C.C.

At five o'clock on the opening day, the M.C.C. had assembled, all except the Pea, for whom Rajam was waiting anxiously. He had promised to bring the real stumps. It was half an hour past time and yet he was not to be seen anywhere.

At last his puny figure was discovered in the distance. There was a catch in Rajam's heart when he saw him. He strained his eyes to find out if the Pea had the things about him. But since the latter was coming from the west, he was seen in the blaze of the evening sun. All the twelve assembled in the field shaded their eyes and looked. Some said that he was carrying a bundle, while some thought that he was swinging his hands freely.

When he arrived, Rajam asked, "Why didn't you tell us that you hadn't the stumps?"

"I have still got them," protested the Pea, "I shall bring them tomorrow. I am sure my father knows where they are kept."

"You kept us waiting till now. Why did you not come earlier and tell us that you could not find them?"

"I tell you, I have been spending hours looking for them everywhere. How could I come here and tell you and at the same time search?"

A cloud descended upon the gathering. For over twenty hours every one among them had been dreaming of swinging a bat and throwing a ball. And they could have realized the dream but for the Pea's wickedness. Everybody looked at him sourly. He was isolated. Rajam felt like crying when he saw the deal-wood planks and the tennis balls lying useless on the ground. What a glorious evening they could have had if only the stumps had been brought!

Amidst all this gloom somebody cast a ray of light by suggesting that they might use the compound wall of Rajam's bungalow as a temporary wicket.

A portion of the wall was marked off with a piece of charcoal, and the captain arranged the field and opened the batting himself. Swaminathan took up the bowling. He held a tennis ball in his hand, took a few paces, and threw it over. Rajam swung the bat but missed it. The ball hit the wall right under the charcoal mark. Rajam was bowled out with the very first ball! There was a great shout of joy. The players pressed round Swaminathan to shake him and pat him on the back, and he was given on the very spot the title, 'Tate'.

14

GRANNY SHOWS HER IGNORANCE

Work was rather heavy in the Board High School. The amount of homework given at the Albert Mission was nothing compared to the heap given at the Board. Every teacher thought that his was the only subject that the boys had to study. Six sums in arithmetic, four pages of 'handwriting copy', dictionary meanings of scores of tough words, two maps, and five stanzas in Tamil poetry, were the average homework every day. Swaminathan sometimes wished that he had not left his old school. The teachers here were ruthless beings: not to speak of the drill three evenings a week, there were scout classes, compulsory games, et cetera, after the regular hours every day; and missing a single class meant half a dozen cane-cuts on the following day. The wizened spectacled man was a repulsive creature, with his screeching voice; the Head of the Albert Mission had a majestic air about him in spite of all his defects.

All this rigour and discipline resulted in a life with little scope for leisure. Swaminathan got up pretty early, rushed through all his homework, and rose just in time to finish the meal and reach the school as the first bell rang. Every day, as he passed the cloth shop at the end of Market Road, the first bell reached his ears. And just as he panted into the class, the second bell would go off. The bell lacked the rich note of the Albert Mission gong; there was something mean and nasal about it. But he soon got accustomed to it.

Except for an hour in the afternoon, he had to be glued to his seat right on till four-thirty in the evening. He had lost the last-bench habit (it might be because he no longer had Mani's company in the classroom). He sat in the second row, and no dawdling easy-going nonsense was tolerated there; you sat right under the teacher's nose. When the four-thirty bell rang, Swaminathan slipped his pencil into his pocket and stretched his cramped aching fingers.

The four-thirty bell held no special thrill. You could not just dash out of the class with a howl of joy. You had to go to the drill ground and stand in a solemn line, and for three-quarters of an hour the drill master treated you as if you were his dog. He drove you to march left and right, stand attention, and swing the arms, or climb the horizontal or parallel bars, whether you liked it or not, whether you knew the thing or not.

For aught the drill master cared, you might lose your balance on the horizontal bars and crack your skull.

At the end of this you ran home to drink coffee, throw down the books, and rush off to the cricket field which was a long way off. You covered the distance half running, half walking, moved by the vision of a dun field sparsely covered with scorched grass, lit into a blaze by the slant rays of the evening sun, enveloped in a flimsy cloud of dust, alive with the shouts of players stamping about. What music there was in the thud of the bat hitting the ball! Just as you took the turn leading to Lawley Extension, you looked at the sun, which stood poised like a red-hot coin on the horizon. You hoped it would not sink. But by the time you arrived at the field the sun went down, leaving only a splash of colour and light in the sky. The shadows already crept out, and one or two municipal lanterns twinkled here and there. You still hoped you would be in time for a good game. But from about half a furlong away you saw the team squatting carelessly round the field. Somebody was wielding the bat rather languidly, bowled and fielded by a handful who were equally languid—the languor that comes at the end of a strenuous evening in the sun.

In addition to the misery of disappointment, you found Rajam a bit sore. He never understood the difficulties of a man. "Oh, Swami, why are you late again?"

"Wretched drill class."

"Oh damn your drill classes and scout classes! Why don't you come early?"

"What can I do, Rajam? I can't help it."

"Well, well. I don't care. You are always ready with excuses. Since the new bats, balls and things arrived, you have hardly played four times."

Others being too tired to play, eventually you persuaded the youngest member of the team (a promising, obedient boy of the Fifth Standard, who was admitted because he cringed and begged Rajam perseveringly) to bowl while you batted. And when you tired of it, you asked him to hold the bat and started bowling, and since you were the Tate of the team, the youngster was rather nervous. And again you took up batting, and then bowling, and so on. It went on till it became difficult to find the ball in the semi-darkness and the picker ran after small dark objects on the ground, instead of after the ball. At this stage a rumour started that the ball was lost and caused quite a stir. The figures squatting and reposing got busy, and the ball was retrieved. After this the captain passed an order forbidding further play, and the stumps were drawn for the day, and soon all the players melted in the darkness. You stayed behind with Rajam and Mani, perched upon Rajam's compound wall, and discussed the day's game and the players, noting the improvement, stagnation, or degeneration of each player, till it became quite dark and a peon came to inform Rajam that his tutor had come.

***

One evening, returning from the cricket field, after parting from Mani at the Grove Street junction, Swaminathan's conscience began to trouble him. A slight incident had happened during the early evening when he had gone home from the school to throw down the books and start for the cricket field. He had just thrown down the books and was running towards the kitchen when Granny cried, "Swami, Swami. Oh, boy, come here."

"No," he said as usual and was in a moment out of her sight, in the kitchen, violently sucking coffee out of a tumbler. He could still hear her shaky querulous voice calling him. There was something appealing in that weak voice, and he had a fit of pity for her sitting and calling people who paid no heed to her. As soon as he had drunk the coffee, he went to her and asked, "What do you want?"

She looked up and asked him to sit down. At that he lost his temper and all the tenderness he had felt for her a moment back. He raved, "If you are going to, say what you have to say as quickly as possible...If not, don't think I am a silly fool..."

She said, "I shall give you six paise. You can take three paise and bring me a lemon for three paise." She had wanted to open this question slowly and diplomatically, because she knew what to expect from her grandson. And when she asked him to sit down, she did it as the first diplomatic move.

Without condescending to say yes or no, Swaminathan held out his hand for the coins and took them. Granny said, "You must come before I count ten." This imposition of a time-limit irritated him. He threw down the coins and said, "If you want it so urgently, you had better go and get it yourself." It was nearing five-thirty and he wanted to be in the field before sunset. He stood frowning at her as if giving her the choice of his getting the lemon late when he returned from the field, or not at all. She said, "I have a terrible pain in the stomach. Please run out and come back, boy." He did not stay there to hear more.

But now, all the excitement and exhilaration of the play being over, and having bidden the last 'good night', he stood in the Grove and Vinayaka Mudali Street junction, as it were face to face with his soul. He thought of his grandmother and felt guilty. Probably she was writhing with pain at that very moment. It stung his heart as he remembered her pathetic upturned face and watery eyes. He called himself a sneak, a thief, an ingrate, and a hard-hearted villain.

In this mood of self-reproach he reached home. He softly sat beside Granny and kept looking at her. It was contrary to his custom. Every evening as soon as he reached home he would dash straight into the kitchen and worry the cook. But now he felt that his hunger did not matter.

Granny's passage had no light. It had only a shaft falling from the lamp in the hall. In the half-darkness, he could not see her face clearly. She lay still. Swaminathan was seized with a horrible passing doubt whether she might not be dead—of stomach-ache. He controlled his voice and asked, "Granny, how is your pain?"

Granny stirred, opened her eyes, and said, "Swami, you have come! Have you had your food?"

"Not yet. How is your stomach-ache, Granny?"

"Oh, it is all right. It is all right."

It cost him all his mental powers to ask without flinching, "Did you get the lemon?" He wanted to know it. He had been feeling genuinely anxious about it. Granny answered this question at once, but to Swaminathan it seemed an age—a terrible stretch of time during which anything might happen, she might say anything, scold him, disown him, swear that she would have nothing more to do with him, or say reproachfully that if only he had cared to go and purchase the lemon in time he might have saved her, and that she was going to die in a few minutes. But she simply said, "You did right in not going. Your mother had kept a dozen in the kitchen."

Swaminathan was overjoyed to hear this good news. And he expressed this mood of joy in: "You know what my new name is? I am Tate."

"What?"

"Tate."

"What is Tate?" she asked innocently. Swaminathan's disappointment was twofold: she had not known anything of his new title, and failed to understand its rich significance even when told. At other times he would have shouted at her. But now he was a fresh penitent, and so asked her kindly, "Do you mean to say that you don't know Tate?"

"I don't know what you mean."

"Tate, the great cricket player, the greatest bowler on earth. I hope you know what cricket is."

"What is that?" Granny asked. Swaminathan was aghast at this piece of illiteracy. "Do you mean to say, Granny, that you don't know what cricket is, or are you fooling me?"

"I don't know what you mean."

"Don't keep on saying 'I don't know what you mean'. I wonder what the boys and men of your days did in the evenings! I think they spent all the twenty-four hours in doing holy things."

He considered for a second. Here was his granny stagnating in appalling ignorance; and he felt it his duty to save her. He delivered a short speech setting forth the principles, ideals, and the philosophy of the game of cricket, mentioning the radiant gods of that world. He asked her every few seconds if she understood, and she nodded her head, though she caught only three per cent of what he said. He concluded the speech with a sketch of the history and the prospects of the M.C.C. "But for Rajam, Granny," he said, "I don't know where we should have been. He has spent hundreds of rupees on this team. Buying bats and balls is no joke. He has plenty of money in his box. Our team is known even to the Government. If you like, you may write a letter to the M.C.C. and it will be delivered to us promptly. You will see us winning all the cups in Malgudi, and in course of time we shall show even the Madras fellows what cricket is." He added a very important note: "Don't imagine all sorts of fellows can become players in our team."

His father stood behind him, with the baby in his arms. He asked, "What are you lecturing about, young man?"

Swaminathan had not noticed his father's presence, and now writhed awkwardly as he answered, "Nothing... Oh, nothing, Father."

"Come on. Let me know it too."

"It is nothing—Granny wanted to know something about cricket and I was explaining it to her."

"Indeed! I never knew Mother was a sportswoman. Mother, I hope Swami has filled you with cricket-wisdom."

Granny said, "Don't tease the boy. The child is so fond of me. Poor thing! He has been trying to tell me all sorts of things. You are not in the habit of explaining things to me. You are all big men..."

Father replied, pointing at the baby, "Just wait a few days and this little fellow will teach you all the philosophy and the politics in the world." He gently clouted the baby's fat cheeks, and the baby gurgled and chirped joyfully. "He has already started lecturing. Listen attentively, Mother." Granny held up her arms for the baby. But Father clung to him tight and said, "No. No. I came home early only for this fellow's sake. I can't. Come on, Swami, I think we had better sit down for food. Where is your mother?"

***

The captain sternly disapproved Swaminathan's ways. "Swami, I must warn you. You are neglecting the game. You are not having any practice at all."

"It is this wretched Board School work."

"Who asked you to go and join it? They never came and invited you. Never mind. But let me tell you. Even Bradman, Tate, and everybody spends four to five hours on the pitch every day, practising, practising. Do you think you are greater than they?"

"Captain, listen to me. I do my best to arrive at the field before five. But this wretched Board High School timetable is peculiar."

A way out had to be found. The captain suggested, "You must see your headmaster and ask him to exempt you from extra work till the match is over." It was more easily said than done and Swaminathan said so, conjuring up before his mind a picture of the wizened face and the small dingy spectacles of his headmaster.

"I am afraid to ask that monster," Swaminathan said. "He may detain me in Second Form for ages."

"Indeed! Are you telling me that you are in such terror of your headmaster? Suppose I see him?"

"Oh, please don't, captain. I beg you. You don't know what a vicious being he is. He may not treat you well. Even if he behaves well before you, he is sure to kill me when you are gone."

"What is the matter with you, Swami? Your head is full of nonsense. How are we to go on? It is two months since we started the team, and you have not played even for ten days..."

Mani, who had stretched himself on the compound wall, now broke in: "Let us see what your headmaster can do. Let him say yes or no. If he kills you I will pulp him. My clubs have had no work for a long time."

There was no stopping Rajam. The next day he insisted that he would see the headmaster at the school. He would not mind losing a couple of periods of his own class. Mani offered to go with him but was advised to mind his business.

Next morning at nine-thirty Swaminathan spent five minutes rubbing his eyes red, and then complained of headache. His father felt his temples and said that he would be all right if he dashed a little cold water on his forehead.

"Yes, Father," Swaminathan said and went out. He stood outside Father's room and decided that if cold water was a cure for headache he would avoid it, since he was praying for that malady just then. Rajam was coming to see the headmaster, and it would be unwise to go to the school that morning. He went in and asked, "Father, did you say cold water?"

"Yes."

"But don't you think it will give me pneumonia or something? I am also feeling feverish."

Father felt his pulse and said, "Now run to school and you will be all right." It was easier to squeeze milk out of a stone than to get permission from Father to keep away from school.

He whispered into his granny's ear, "Granny, even if I die, I am sure Father will insist on sending my corpse to the school." Granny protested vehemently against this sentiment.

"Granny, a terrible fever is raging within me and my head is splitting with headache. But yet, I mustn't keep away from school."

Granny said, "Don't go to school." She then called Mother and said, "This child has fever. Why should he go to school?"

"Has he?" Mother asked anxiously, and fussed over him. She felt his body and said that he certainly had a temperature. Swaminathan said pathetically, "Give me milk or something, Mother. It is getting late for school." Mother vetoed this virtuous proposal. Swaminathan faintly said, "But Father may not like it." She asked him to lie down on a bed and hurried along to Father's room. She stepped into the room with the declaration, "Swami has fever, and he can't go to school."

"Did you take his temperature?"

"Not yet. It doesn't matter if he misses the school for a day."

"Anyway, take his temperature," he said. He feared that his wife might detect the sarcasm in his suggestion, and added as a palliative, "That we may know whether a doctor is necessary."

A thermometer stuck out of Swaminathan's mouth for half a minute and indicated normal. Mother looked at it and thrust it back into his mouth. It again showed normal. She took it to Father, and he said, "Well, it is normal," itching to add, "I knew it." Mother insisted, "Something has gone wrong with the thermometer.

The boy has fever. There is no better thermometer than my hand. I can swear that he has 100.2 now."

"Quite likely," Father said.

And Swaminathan, when he ought to have been at school, was lying peacefully, with closed eyes, on his bed. He heard a footstep near his bed and opened his eyes. Father stood over him and said in an undertone, "You are a lucky fellow. What a lot of champions you have in this house when you don't want to go to school!" Swaminathan felt that this was a sudden and unprovoked attack from behind. He shut his eyes and turned towards the wall with a feeble groan.

By the afternoon he was already bedsore. He dreaded the prospect of staying in bed through the evening. Moreover, Rajam would have already come to the school in the morning and gone.

He went to his mother and informed her that he was starting for the school. There was a violent protest at once. She felt him all over and said that he was certainly better but in no condition to go to school. Swaminathan said, "I am feeling quite fit, Mother. Don't get fussy."

On the way to the school he met Rajam and Mani. Mani had his club under his arm. Swaminathan feared that these two had done something serious.

Rajam said, "You are a fine fellow! Where were you this morning?"

"Did you see the headmaster, Rajam?"

"Not yet. I found that you had not come, and did not see him. I want you to be with me when I see him. After all it is your business."

When Swaminathan emerged from the emotional chaos which followed Rajam's words, he asked, "What is Mani doing here?"

"I don't know," Rajam said, "I found him outside your school with his club, when he ought to have been in his class."

"Mani, what about your class?"

"It is all right," Mani replied, "I didn't attend it today."

"And why your club?" Swaminathan asked.

"Oh! I simply brought it along."

Rajam asked, "Weren't you told yesterday to attend your class and mind your business?"

"I don't remember. You asked me to mind my business only when I offered to accompany you. I am not accompanying you. I just came this way, and you have also come this way. This is a public road." Mani's jest was lost on them. Their minds were too busy with plans for the impending interview.

"Don't worry, young men," Mani said, "I shall see you through your troubles. I will talk to the headmaster, if you like."

"If you step into his room, he will call the police," Swaminathan said.

When they reached the school Mani was asked to go away, or at worst wait in the road. Rajam went in, and Swaminathan was compelled to accompany him to the headmaster's room.

The headmaster was sleeping with his head between his hands and his elbows resting on the table. It was a small stuffy room with only one window opening on the weather-beaten side wall of a shop; it was cluttered with dust-laden rolls of maps, globes, and geometrical squares. The headmaster's white cane lay on the table across two ink-bottles and some pads. The sun came in a hot dusty beam and fell on the headmaster's nose and the table. He was gently snoring. This was a possibility that Rajam had not thought of.

"What shall we do?" Swaminathan asked in a rasping whisper.

"Wait," Rajam ordered.

They waited for ten minutes and then began to make gentle noises with their feet. The headmaster opened his eyes and without taking his head from his hands, kept staring at them vacantly, without showing any sign of recognition. He rubbed his eyes, raised his eyebrows three times, yawned, and asked in a voice thick with sleep, "Have you fellows no class?" He fumbled for his spectacles and put them on. Now the picture was complete—wizened face and dingy spectacles calculated to strike terror into the hearts of Swaminathans. He asked again, "To what class do you fellows belong? Have you no class?"

"I don't belong to your school," Rajam said defiantly.

"Ah, then which heaven do you drop from?"

Rajam said, "I am the captain of the M.C.C. and have come to see you on business."

"What is that?"

"This is my friend W. S. Swaminathan of Second C studying in your school…"

"I am honoured to meet you," said the headmaster turning to Swaminathan. Rajam felt at that moment that he had found out where the Board High School got its reputation from.

"I am the captain of the M.C.C."

"Equally honoured…"

"He is in my team. He is a good bowler…"

"Are you?" said the headmaster, turning to Swaminathan.

"May I come to the point?" Rajam asked.

"Do, do," said the headmaster, "for heaven's sake, do."

"It is this," Rajam said, "he is a good bowler and he needs some practice. He can't come to the field early enough because he is kept in the school every day after four-thirty."

"What do you want me to do?"

"Sir, can't you permit him to go home after four-thirty?"

The headmaster sank back in his chair and remained silent.

Rajam asked again, "What do you say, sir, won't you do it?"

"Are you the headmaster of this school or am I?"

"Of course you are the headmaster, sir. In Albert Mission they don't keep us a minute longer than four-thirty. And we are exempted from drill if we play games."

"Here I am not prepared to listen to your rhapsodies on that pariah school. Get out."

Mani, who had been waiting outside, finding his friends gone too long, and having his own fears, now came into the headmaster's room.

"Who is this?" asked the headmaster, looking at Mani sourly. "What do you want?"

"Nothing," Mani replied and quietly stood in a corner.

"I can't understand why every fellow who finds nothing to do comes and stands in my room."

"I am the Police Superintendent's son," Rajam said abruptly.

"Is that so? Find out from your father what he was doing on the day a gang of little rascals came in and smashed these windows... What is the thing that fellow has in his hand?"

"My wooden club," Mani answered.

Rajam added, "He breaks skulls with it. Come out, Mani, come on, Swami. There is nothing doing with this—this madcap."

15

BEFORE THE MATCH

The M.C.C.'s challenge to a 'friendly' match was accepted by the Young Men's Union, who kept themselves in form by indefatigable practice on the vacant site behind the Reading Room, or when the owner of this site objected, right in the middle of Kulam Street. The match was friendly in nought but name. The challenge sent by the M.C.C. was couched in terms of defiance and threat.

There were some terrifying conditions attached to the challenge. The first condition was that the players should be in the field promptly at eleven o'clock. The second was that they should carry their own bats, while the stumps would be graciously supplied by the M.C.C. The third was not so much a plain condition as a firm hint that they would do well to bring and keep in stock a couple of their own balls. The reason for this was given in the pithy statement 'that your batsmen might hit your own balls and not break ours'. The next was the inhospitable suggestion that they had better look out for themselves in regard to lunch, if they cared to have any at all. The last condition was perhaps the most complicated of the lot, over which some argument and negotiation ensued: 'You shall pay for breaking bats, balls, wickets, and other damages.'

The Y.M.U. captain was rather puzzled by this. He felt that it was irrelevant in view of the fact that there were conditions 2 and 3, and if they broke any bats and balls at all, it would be their own property and the M.C.C.'s anxiety to have the damage made good was unwarranted. He was told that the stumps belonged to the M.C.C. anyway, and there was also the Y.M.U.'s overlooking clauses 2 and 3. At which the Y.M.U. captain became extremely indignant and asked why if the M.C.C. was so impoverished, it should not come and play in their (Y.M.U.'s) own pitch and save them the trouble of carrying their team about. The stinging rejoinder occurred to the indignant Rajam exactly twenty minutes after the other captain had left, that it could not be done as the M.C.C. did not think much of a match played in the middle of Kulam Street, if the owner of the vacant site behind the Reading Room should take it into his head to object to the match. Before he left, the Y.M.U. captain demanded to be told what 'other damages' in the last clause meant. Rajam paused, looked about, and pointed to the windows and tiles of a house adjoining the M.C.C. field.

The match was to be played on Sunday two weeks later.

Rajam lost all peace of mind. He felt confident that his team could thrash the Y.M.U. He himself could be depended upon not to let down the team. Mani was steady if unimpressive. He could be depended upon to stop with his head, if necessary, any ball. His batting was not bad. He had a peculiar style. With his bat he stopped all reasonable approaches to the wicket and brought the best bowlers to a fainting condition. Rajam did not consider it worth while to think of the other players of the team. There was only one player who caused him the deepest anxiety day and night. He was a dark horse. On him rested a great task, a mighty responsibility. He was the Tate of the team, and he must bowl out all the eleven of the other team. But he looked uncertain. Even with the match only a fortnight off, he did not seem to care for practice. He stuck to his old habit of arriving at the field when darkness had fallen on the earth. "Swami," Rajam pleaded, "please do try to have at least an hour's practice in the evenings."

"Certainly Rajam, if you can suggest a way..."

"Why not you tell your headmaster that..."

"Oh, no, no," Swaminathan cried, "I am grateful to you for your suggestion. But let us not think of that man. He has not forgotten your last visit yet."

"I don't care. What I want is that you should have good practice. If you keep any batsman standing for more than five minutes, I will never see your face again. You needn't concern yourself with the score. You can leave it to us..."

***

Just seven days before the match, Swaminathan realized that his evenings were more precious than ever. As soon as the evening bell rang, he lined up with the rest in the drill ground. But contrary to the custom, he had not taken off his coat and cap. All the others were in their shirts, with their *dhotis* tucked up. The drill master, a square man with protruding chest, a big moustache sharpened at the ends, and a silk turban wound in military style, stood as if he posed before a camera, and surveyed his pupils with a disdainful side-glance. The monitor called out the names from the greasy register placed on the vaulting-horse. The attendance after an interminable time was over and the drill master gave up his pose, came near the file, and walked from one end to the other, surveying each boy sternly. Swaminathan being short came towards the end of the file. The drill master stopped before him, looked him up and down and passed on muttering: "You won't get leave. Coat and cap off."

Swaminathan became desperate and pursued him: "Sir, I am in a terrible state of health. I can't attend drill today. I shall die if I do. Sir, I think I shall—" He was prancing behind the drill master.

The drill master had come to the last boy and yet Swaminathan was dogging him. He turned round on Swaminathan with a fierce oath: "What is the matter with you?"

"Sir, you don't understand my troubles. You don't even care to ask me what I am suffering from."

"Yes, yes, what exactly is ailing you now?"

Swaminathan had at first thought of complaining of headache, but now he saw that the drill master was in a mood to slight even the most serious of headaches. He had an inspiration and said: "Sir, the whole of last night I was delirious."

The drill master was stunned by this piece of news. "You were delirious! Are you mad?"

"No, sir. I didn't sleep a wink last night. I was delirious. Our doctor said so. He has asked me not to attend drill for a week to come. He said that I should die if I attended drill."

"Get away, young swine, before I am tempted to throttle you. I don't believe a word. But you are a persevering swine. Get out."

The intervening period, about half an hour, between leaving the drill ground and reaching the cricket field, was a blur of hurry and breathlessness. Everybody at the field was happy to see him so early. Rajam jumped with joy.

On the whole everything was satisfactory. The only unpleasant element in all this was an obsession that the drill master might spy him out. So that, when they dispersed for the evening, Swaminathan stayed in Rajam's house till it was completely dark and then skulked home, carefully avoiding the lights falling in the street from shop-fronts.

The next morning he formed a plan to be free all the evenings of the week. He was at his desk with the *Manual of Grammar* open before him. It was seven-thirty in the morning, and he had still two and a half hours before him for the school.

He did a little cautious reconnoitring: Mother was in the baby's room, for the rhythmic creaking of the cradle came to his ears. Father's voice was coming from the front room; he was busy with his clients. Swaminathan quietly slipped out of the house.

He stood before a shop in front of which hung the board: "Doctor T. Kesavan, L. M. & S. Sri Krishna Dispensary." The doctor was sitting at a long table facing the street. Swaminathan found that the doctor was alone and free, and entered the shop.

"Hallo, Swaminathan, what is the matter?"

"Nothing, sir. I have come on a little business."

"All well at home?"

"Quite. Doctor, I have got to have a doctor's certificate immediately."

"What is the matter with you?"

"I will tell you the truth, doctor. I have to play a match next week against the Young Men's Union. And I must have some practice. And yet every evening there is drill class, scouting, some dirty period or other. If you could give me a certificate asking them to let me off at four-thirty, it would help the M.C.C. to win the match."

"Well, I could do it. But is there anything wrong with you?"

Swaminathan took half a second to find an answer: "Certainly, I am beginning to feel of late that I have delirium."

"What did you say?" asked the doctor anxiously.

Swaminathan was pleased to find the doctor so much impressed, and repeated that he was having the most violent type of delirium.

"Boy, did you say delirium? What exactly do you mean by delirium?"

Swaminathan did not consider it the correct time for cross-examination. But he had to have the doctor's favour. He answered: "I have got it. I can't say exactly. But it isn't some, some kind of stomach-ache?"

The doctor laughed till a great fit of coughing threatened to choke him. After that he looked Swaminathan under the eye, examined his tongue, tapped his chest, and declared him to be in the pink of health, and told him he would do well to stick to his drill if he wanted to get rid of delirium. Swaminathan again explained to him how important it was for him to have his evenings free. But the doctor said: "It is all very well. But I should be prosecuted if I gave you any such certificate."

"Who is going to find it out, doctor? Do you want our M.C.C. to lose the match?"

"I wish you all success. Don't worry. I can't give you a certificate. But I shall talk to your headmaster about you and request him to let you off after four-thirty."

"That will do. You are very kind to me, doctor."

***

At four-thirty that evening, without so much as thinking of the scouting class in the quadrangle of the school, Swaminathan went home and then to the cricket field. Next day he had drill class, and he did not give it a thought. He was having plenty of practice. Rajam said: "Swami, you are wonderful! All that you needed was a little practice. What have you done about your evening classes?"

"It is a slight brainwave, my boy. Our doctor has told the headmaster that I should die if I stayed in the school after four-thirty. I got him to do it. What do you think of it?"

Mani dug him in the ribs and cried: "You are the brainiest fellow I have ever seen." Rajam agreed with him, and then was suddenly seized with worry: "Oh, I don't know if we shall win that match. I will die if we lose."

Mani said: "Here, Rajam, I am sick of your talks of defeat. Do you think those monkey-faced fools can stand up to us?"

"I shall write to the papers if we win," said Rajam.

"Will they print our photos?" Tate asked.

"Without doubt."

***

It was during the geography hour on Friday that the headmaster came to the class, cane in hand. The geography master, Mr Rama Rao, a mild elderly person, rose respectfully. The headmaster gave the full benefit of his wizened face to the class. His owl-like eyes were fixed upon Swaminathan, and he said: "Get up."

Swaminathan got up.

"Come here."

Swaminathan 'came' there promptly.

"Show your shameless face to the class fully."

Swaminathan now tried to hide his face. The headmaster threw out his arm and twisted Swaminathan's neck to make him face the class, and said: "This great man is too busy to bother about such trivial matters as drill and scouting, and has not honoured these classes with his presence since last Monday." His lips twisted in a wry smile. The class considered it safer to take the cue, and gently giggled. Even on the geography master's face there appeared a polite smile.

"Sir, have you any explanation to give?" the headmaster asked.

With difficulty Swaminathan found his voice and answered: "It was the doctor—didn't the doctor talk to you about me, sir?"

"What doctor talk about what?"

"He said he would," faintly answered Swaminathan.

"If you talk in enigmas I shall strip you before the class and thrash you."

"Dr Kesavan said—"

"What about Dr Kesavan?"

"He said he would talk to you about me and get me exemption from drill and other extra periods. He said that I should die if I attended drill for some days to come."

"And pray what is your trouble?"

"He thinks it is some—some kind—of—delirium you know." He had determined to avoid this word since he met the doctor last, but at this critical moment he blundered into it by sheer habit.

The headmaster turned to the teacher and raised his brow. He waited for some time and said: "I am waiting to hear what other words of truth and wisdom are going to drop from your mouth."

"Sir, I thought he had talked to you. He said he would..."

"I don't care to have every street mongrel come and tell me what to do in my school with my boys. It is a good thing that this surgeon-general did not come. If he had, I would have asked the peon to bash his head on the table."

Swaminathan realized that the doctor had deceived him. He remembered the genial smile with which the doctor had said that he would see the headmaster. Swaminathan shuddered as he realized what a deep-dyed villain Dr Kesavan was behind that genial smile. He would teach that villain a lesson, put a snake into his table-drawer; he would not allow that villain to feel his pulse even if he (Swaminathan) should be dying of fever.

Further plans of revenge were stopped by a flick of the cane on his knuckles. The headmaster held the cane ready and cried: "Hold out your hand. Six on each hand for each day of absence, and the whole of the next lesson on the bench. Monitor, you had better see to it. And remember, W. S. Swaminathan, if you miss a single class again, I shall strip you in the school hall and ask the peon to cane you. You can't frighten me with your superintendents of police, their sons, grandsons, or grandfathers. I don't care even if you complain to His Majesty". He released Swaminathan's neck and raised the cane.

Another moment and that vicious snake-like cane, quivering as if with life, would have descended on Swaminathan's palm. A flood of emotion swept him off his feet, a mixture of fear, resentment, and rage. He hardly knew what he was doing. His arm shot out, plucked the cane from the headmaster's hand, and flung it out of the window. Then he dashed to his desk, snatched his books, and ran out of the room. He crossed the hall and the veranda in a run, climbed the school gate because the bolt was too heavy for him, and jumped into the end of Market Road.

He sat under a tree on the roadside to collect his thoughts. He had left the school to which he would never go back as long as that tyrant was there. If his father should hear of it, he would do heaven knew what. He would force him to go back, which would be impossible... He had got out of two schools in this fashion. There were no more schools in Malgudi. His father would have to send him to Trichinopoly or Madras. But probably the Board High School headmaster would write to all the schools, telling them who Swaminathan was. He would not be admitted to

any school. So he would have to work and earn... He
might get some rupees—and he could go to hotels
and buy coffee and tiffin as often as he pleased. What
divine sweets the Bombay Anand Bhavan made! There
was some green slab on the top left of the stall, with
almonds stuck on it. He had always wanted to eat it,
but lacked the courage to ask the hotel man, as he
believed it to be very costly... His father would not
allow him to remain in the house if he did not go to
school. He might beat him. He would not go home
that day nor on any other day. He could not face his
father. He wondered at the same time where he could
go. Anywhere. If he kept walking along Market Road
where would it lead him? Probably to Madras. Could
he reach Bombay and England if he went further? He
could work in any of those places, earn money and do
what he pleased. If he should go by train... But what
to do for money? There might not be much trouble
about that. The station-master was an amiable man
and Swaminathan knew him.

The school bell rang, and Swaminathan rose to
hurry away. The boys might come out, stand around,
and watch him as if he were something funny.

He hurried along Market Road, turned to his right,
along Smith Street, and taking a short cut through some
intricate lanes, stood before his old school, the Albert
Mission. The sight of the deep yellow building with
its top storey filled him with a nostalgia for old times.
He wished he had not left it. How majestic everything
there now seemed! The headmaster, so dignified in
his lace-turban, so unlike the grubby wretch of the

Board. Vedanayagam, Ebenezar—even Ebenezar. D. P. Pillai, how cosy and homely his history classes were! Swaminathan almost wept at the memory of Somu and Pea…All his friends were there, Rajam, Somu, Mani, and the Pea, happy, dignified, and honoured within the walls of the august Albert Mission School. He alone was out of it, isolated, as if he were a leper. He was an outcast, an outcast. He was filled with a sudden self-disgust. Oh, what would he not give to be back in the old school! Only, they would not take him in. It was no use. He had no more schools to go to in Malgudi. He must run away to Madras and work. But he had better see Rajam and Mani before going away.

He lingered outside the school gate. He had not the courage to enter it. He was the enemy of the school. The peon Singaram might assault him and drive him out if he saw him. He discreetly edged close to the massive concrete gatepost which screened him from a direct view of the school. He had to meet Rajam and Mani. But how? He stood still for a few minutes and formed a plan.

He went round behind the school. It was a part of the building that nobody frequented. It was a portion of the fallow field adjoining the school and terminating in the distant railway embankment. Swaminathan had not seen this place even once in all the six or seven years that he had spent at the school. Here the school compound wall was half covered with moss, and the rear view of the school was rather interesting. From here Swaminathan could see only the top half of the building, but even that presented a curious appearance.

For instance, he could not at once point out where his old Second A was situated. He rolled up a stone to the foot of the wall, and stood on it. He could just see the school compound now. It was about twelve, the busiest hour in the school, and there was not a single person in the compound. He waited. It was tedious waiting. After a short time, a very small person came out of the First Standard, to blow his nose. The three sections of the First Standard were in a block not a dozen yards from Swaminathan.

Swaminathan whistled softly, and the very small person did not hear. Swaminathan repeated the whistling, and the very small person turned and started as if he saw an apparition. Swaminathan beckoned to him. The small person took just a second to decide whether to obey the call of that apparition or to run back to the class. Swaminathan called him again. And the very small man drew towards him as if in a hypnotic state, staring wildly.

Swaminathan said: "Would you like to have an almond peppermint?"

The very small man could hardly believe his ears. Here was a man actually offering almond peppermints! It could not be true. There was probably some fraud in it. Swaminathan repeated the offer and the small man replied rather cautiously that he would like to have the peppermint.

"Well, then," Swaminathan said, "you can't have it just now. You will have to earn it. Just go to Second Form A and tell M. Rajam that somebody from his house wants him urgently and bring him over here, and then hold out your hand for the peppermint. Maybe you will be given two."

The small man stood silent, assimilating every detail of the question and then with a puckered brow asked: "Where is Second Form A?"

"Upstairs."

"Oh!" the boy ejaculated with a note of despair, and stood ruminating.

"What do you say?" Swaminathan asked, and added: "Answer me before I count ten. Otherwise the offer is off. One, two, three—"

"You say it is upstairs?" the boy asked.

"Of course I do."

"But I have never gone there."

"You will have to now."

"I don't know the way."

"Just climb the stairs."

"They may—they may beat me if I am seen there."

"If you care for the almond peppermint you will have to risk it. Say at once whether you will go or not."

"All right. Wait for me." The very small man was off.

Ten minutes later he returned, followed by Rajam. Rajam was astonished to see Swaminathan's head over the wall. "What are you doing here?"

"Jump over the wall. I want you very urgently, Rajam."

"I have got a class. I can't come out now."

"Don't be absurd. Come on. I have something very urgent to say."

Rajam jumped over the wall and was by his side.

Swaminathan's head disappeared from view. A pathetic small voice asked over the wall: "Where is my peppermint?"

"Oh, I forgot you, little one," Swaminathan said, reappearing, "come on, catch this." He tossed a three-paisa coin at the other.

"You said almond peppermint," the boy reminded.

"I may say a thousand things," Swaminathan answered brusquely, "but isn't a three-paisa coin sufficient? You can buy an almond peppermint if you want."

"But you said two almond peppermints."

"Now be off, young man. Don't haggle with me like a brinjal seller. Learn contentment," said Swaminathan and jumped down from the stone.

"Rajam, do you know what has happened in the school today? I have fought with the headmaster. I am dismissed. I have no more schools or classes."

"You fought with the headmaster?"

"Yes, he came to assault me about the drill attendance, and I wrenched his hand, and snatched the cane...I don't believe I shall ever go back to the school. I expect there will be a lot of trouble if I do."

"What a boy you are!" exclaimed Rajam. "You are always in some trouble or other wherever you go. Always, always—"

"It was hardly my fault, Rajam," Swaminathan said, and tried to vindicate himself by explaining to him Dr Kesavan's villainy.

"You have no sense, Swami. You are a peculiar fellow."

"What else could I do to get the evenings off for practice? The Y.M.U. are no joke."

"You are right, Swami. I watched the fellows at practice this morning. They have morning practice too. They are not bad players. There is one Mohideen, a dark fellow, oh, you know—you will have to keep an eye on him. He bats like Bradman. You will have to watch him. There is another fellow, Shanmugam. He is a dangerous bowler. But there is one weakness in Mohideen. He is not so steady on the leg side...Swami, don't worry about anything for some time to come. You must come in the morning too tomorrow. We have got to beat those fellows."

Swaminathan had really called Rajam to bid him goodbye, but now he changed his mind. Rajam would stop him if he came to know of his adventurous plans. He wasn't going to tell Rajam or anybody about it, not even Mani. If he was stopped, he would have no place to stay in. The match was still two days off. He would go away without telling anyone, somehow practise on the way, come back for a few hours on the day of the match, disappear once again, and never come back to Malgudi—a place which contained his father, a stern stubborn father, and that tyrant of a headmaster... And no amount of argument on his part could ever make his father see eye to eye with him. If he went home, Father might beat him, thrash him, or kill him, to make him return to the Board High School. Father was a tough man... He would have to come back on the day of the match, without anybody's knowledge. Perhaps it would not be necessary. He asked suddenly: "Rajam, do you think I am so necessary for the match?"

Rajam regarded him suspiciously and said: "Don't ask such questions." He added presently: "We can't do without you, Swami. No. We depend upon you. You are the best bowler we have. We have got to give those fellows a beating. I shall commit suicide if we lose. Oh, Swami, what a mess you have made of things! What are you going to do without a school?"

"I shall have to join a workshop or some such thing."

"What will your father say when he hears of it?"

"Oh, nothing. He will say it is all right. He won't trouble me," Swaminathan said.

"Swami, I must get back to the class. It is late." Rajam rose and sprinted towards the school, crying: "Come to the field early. Come very soon, now that you are free..."

16

SWAMI DISAPPEARS

Swaminathan's father felt ashamed of himself as he approached Ellaman Street, the last street of the town, which turned into a rough track for about a hundred yards and disappeared into the sands of the Sarayu River. He hesitated for a second at the end of Market Road, which was bright with the lights of a couple of late shops and a street gas-lamp, before he turned to plunge into the darkness and silence of Ellaman Street. A shaft of greenish light from the gas-lamp fell athwart Ellaman Street, illuminating only a few yards of the street and leaving the rest in deep gloom. A couple of municipal lanterns smouldered in their wicks, emphasizing the darkness around.

Swaminathan's father felt ashamed of himself. He was going to cross the street, plod through the sand,

and gaze into the Sarayu—for the body of his son! His son, Swami, to be looked for in the Sarayu! It seemed to him a ridiculous thing to do. But what could he do? He dared not return home without some definite news of his son, good or bad. The house had worn a funeral appearance since nine o'clock. His wife and his old mother were more or less dazed and demented. She— his wife—had remained cheerful till the *Taluk* Office gong struck ten, when, her face turning white, she had asked him to go and find out from Swaminathan's friends and teachers what had happened to him.

He did not know where Swaminathan's headmaster lived. He had gone to the Board School and asked the watchman, who misdirected him and made him wander over half the town without purpose. He could not find Mani's house. He had gone to Rajam's house, but the house was dark, everybody had gone to bed, and he felt that it would be absurd to wake up the household of a stranger to ask if they had seen his son. From what he could get out of the servant sleeping in the veranda, he understood that Swaminathan had not been seen in Rajam's house that evening. He had then vaguely wandered in the streets. He was doing it to please his wife and mother. He had not shared in the least his wife's nervousness. He had felt all along that the boy must have gone out somewhere and would return, and then he would treat him with some firmness and nip this tendency in the bud. He had spent nearly an hour thus and gone home. Even his mother had left her bed and was hobbling agitatedly about the house, praying to the God of the Thirupathi Hills and promising him rich offerings if he should restore Swaminathan to her safe and sound. His wife stood like a stone image, looking down the street. The only tranquil being in the house was the youngest member of the family, whose soft breathings came from the cradle, defying the gloom and heaviness in the house.

When Swaminathan's father gave his wife the news—or no news—that he had gathered from his wanderings, he had assumed a heavy aggressive cheerfulness. It had lasted for a while, but gradually the anxiety and the nervousness of the two women infected him. He had begun to feel that something must have happened to his son—a kidnapping or an accident. He was trying to reason out these fears when his wife asked in a trembling voice: "Did you search in the hospital?" and broke into a hysterical cry. He received this question with apparent disdain, while his mind was conjuring up a vision of his son lying in a pulp in the hospital. He was struggling to erase this picture from his mind when his mother made matters worse with the question: "Tell me—tell me—where could the boy have gone? Were you severe with him for anything this morning?"

He was indignant at this question. Everybody seemed to be holding him responsible for Swaminathan's disappearance. Since nine o'clock he had been enduring the sly references and the suspicious glances. But this upset him, and he sharply asked his mother to return to her bed and not to let her brain concoct silly questions. He had after that reviewed his behaviour with his son since the morning, and discovered with surprise and relief that he had not seen him the whole day. The boy had risen from bed, studied, and gone to school, while he had shut himself up in his room with his clients. He then wondered if he had done anything in the past two or three days. He was not certain of his memory, but he felt that his conduct was blameless. As far as he could remember there had not been any word or act of his that could have embittered the boy and make him do—do—wild things.

It was nearing twelve and he found his wife still sobbing. He tried to console her and rose to go out saying, again with a certain loud cheerfulness: "I am going out to look for him. If he comes before I return, for heaven's sake don't let him know what I am out for. I don't care to appear a fool in his eyes."

He had walked rather briskly up Hospital Road, but had turned back after staring at the tall iron gates of the hospital. He told himself that it was unnecessary to enter the hospital, but in fact knew that he lacked the courage. That very window in which a soft dim light appeared might have behind it the cot containing Swaminathan all pulped and bandaged. He briskly moved out of Hospital Road and wandered about rather aimlessly through a few dark lanes around the place. With each hour, his heart became heavier. He had slunk past Market Road, and now entered Ellaman Street.

He swiftly passed through Ellaman Street and crossed the rough footpath leading to the river. His pace slackened as he approached the river. He tried to convince himself that he was about to do a piece of work which was a farce. But if the body of his son, sodden and bloated, should be seen stuck up among the reeds, and rocking gently on the ripples...He shut his eyes and prayed: "Oh, God, help me."

He looked far up and down the river which was gliding along with gentle music. The massive *peepul* trees overhanging the river sighed to the night. He started violently at the sight of the flimsy shadow of some branch on the water; and again as some float kept tilting against the moss-covered parapet with muffled thuds.

And then, still calling himself a fool, he went to the Malgudi Railway Station and walked a mile or so along the railway line, keenly examining the iron rails and the sleepers. The ceaseless hum and the shrill whistle of night insects, the whirring of bats, and the croaking of frogs, came through the awful loneliness of the night. He once stooped with a shudder to put his finger on some wet patch on the rails. As he held up the finger and examined it in the starlight and found that it was only water and not blood, he heaved a sigh of relief and thanked God.

17

THE DAY OF THE MATCH

A narrow road branching to the left of the trunk road attracted Swaminathan because it was shaded by trees bearing fruits. The white ball-like wood-apple, green figs, and the deep purple eugenia peeped out of thick green foliage. He walked a mile and did not like the road. It was utterly deserted and silent. He wished to be back in the trunk road in which there was some life and traffic, though few and far between: some country cart lumbering along; or an occasional motor-car with trunks and bedding strapped behind, whizzing past and disappearing in a cloud of dust; or groups of peasants moving on the edge of the road. But this branch road oppressed him with its stillness. Moreover, he had been wandering for many hours away from home, and now longed to be back there. He became desperate at the thought of home. What fine things the cook prepared! And how Mother always insisted upon serving ghee and curds herself! Oh! how he would sit before his leaf and watch Mother open the cupboard and bring out the aluminium curd-pot, and how soft and white it was as it noiselessly fell on the heap of rice on the leaf and enveloped it! A fierce hunger now raged within him. His thighs were heavy and there was pain around his hips. He did not notice it, but the sun's rays were coming obliquely from the west and the birds were on their homeward flight.

When hunger became unbearable, he plucked and ate fruits. There was a clean pond nearby.

He rested for some time and then started to go back home. The only important thing now was home, and all the rest seemed trivial beside it. The Board School affair appeared inconsequent. He marvelled at himself for having taken it seriously and rushed into all this trouble. What a fool he had been! He wished with all his heart that he had held out his hand when the headmaster raised his cane. Even if he had not done it, he wished he had gone home and told his father everything. Father would have scolded him a little (in case he went too far, Granny and Mother could always be depended upon to come to his rescue). All this scolding and frowning would have been worth while, because Father could be depended upon to get him out of any trouble. People were afraid of him. And what foolishness to forgo practice with the match only two days ahead! If the match was lost, there was no knowing what Rajam would do.

Meanwhile, Swaminathan was going back towards the trunk road. He thought he would be presently back in it, and then he had only to go straight and it would take him right into Market Road, and from there he could reach home blindfold. His parents might get angry with him if he went home so late. But he could tell them that he had lost his way. Or would that be too mild? Suppose he said that he had been kidnapped by *Pathans* and had to escape from them with great difficulty...

He felt he had been walking long enough. He ought to have reached the trunk road long ago, but as he stopped and looked about, he found that he was still going along the thick avenue of figs and wood-apple. The ground was strewn with discoloured, disfigured fruits, and leaves. The road seemed to be longer now that he was going back. The fact was that he had unconsciously followed a gentle imperceptible curve, as the road cunningly branched and joined the Memphis Forest Road. Some seventy miles further it split into a number of rough irregular tracks disappearing into the thick belt of Memphis Forests. If he had just avoided this deceptive curve, he would have reached the trunk road long ago.

Night fell suddenly, and his heart beat fast. His throat went dry as he realized that he had not reached the trunk road. The trees were still thick and the road was still narrow. The trunk road was broader, and there the sky was not screened by branches. But here one could hardly see the sky; the stars gleamed through occasional gaps overhead. He quickened his pace though he was tired. He ran a little distance, his feet falling on the leaf-covered ground with a sharp rustling noise. The birds in the branches overhead started at this noise and fluttered their wings. In that deep darkness and stillness the noise of fluttering wings had an uncanny ghostly quality. Swaminathan was frightened and stood still. He must reach the trunk road and thence find his way home. He would not mind even if it were twelve o'clock when he reached the trunk road. There was something reassuring in its spaciousness and in the sparseness of vegetation. But here the closeness of the tree-trunks and their branches intertwining at the top gave the road the appearance of a black, bleak cavern with an evil spirit brooding over it.

The noise of the disturbed birds subsided. He started on again. He trod warily so as not to make a noise and disturb the birds again, though he felt an urge to run, run with all his might and reach the trunk road and home. The conflict between the impulse to run and the caution that counselled him not to run was fierce. As he walked noiselessly, slowly, suppressing the impulse to run on madly, his nerves quivered with the strain. It was as if he had been rope-walking in a gale.

His ears became abnormally sensitive. They caught every noise his feet made, with the slightest variations. His feet came down on the ground with a light tick or a subdued crackle or a gentle swish, according to the object on the ground: small dry twigs, half-green leaves, or a thick layer of dry withered leaves. There were occasional patches of bare uncovered ground, and there the noise was a light thud, or pit-pat; pit-pat-pit-pat in monotonous repetition. Every noise entered Swaminathan's ears. For some time he was conscious of nothing else. His feet said pish—pish—pish—pat—pit—pat—swish and crackled. These noises streamed into his head, monotonously, endlessly. They were like sinister whispers, calling him to a dreadful sacrifice. He clearly heard his name whispered. There was no doubt about it. "Swami...Swami...Swami...Swami...Swami..." the voice said, and then the dreadful suggestion of a sacrifice. It was some devil, coming behind him noiselessly, and saying the same thing over and over again, deep into his ears. He stopped and looked about. There the immense monster crouched, with its immense black legs wide apart, and its shadowy arms joined over its head. It now swayed a little. He dared not take his eyes off it for fear that it might pounce upon him. He stood frozen to the ground and stared at this monster. Why did it cease its horrid whispers the moment he turned back? He stood staring. He might have spent about five minutes thus. And when the first thrill of fear subsided, he saw a little more clearly and found that the monster consisted of massive tree-trunks and their top branches.

He continued his journey. He was perhaps within a yard of the trunk road, and afterwards he would sing as he sauntered home. He asked himself whether he would rest awhile on the trunk road or go, without stopping, home. His legs felt as if they had been made of stone. He decided that he would sit down for some time when he reached the trunk road. It did not matter. The trunk road was safe and secure even at twelve o'clock. If he took a rest, he would probably be able to run home...

He came to a clearing. The stars were visible above. The road wound faintly in front of him. No brooding darkness, no clustering crowded avenue here. He felt a momentary ecstasy as he realized that he had come to the trunk road. It bore all the characteristics of the trunk road. The sight of the stars above, clear and uninterrupted, revived him. As he paused and watched the million twinkling bodies, he felt like bursting into music out of sheer relief. He had left behind the horrid, narrow, branch-roofed road. At this realization his strength came back to him. He decided not to waste time in resting. He felt fit to go forward. But presently he felt uneasy. He remembered clearly that the branch road began at right angles to the trunk road. But here it continued straight. He stood bewildered for a moment and then told himself that it was probably a continuation of the branch road, a continuation that he had not noticed before. Whatever it was, the trunk road must surely cut this at right angles, and if he turned to his right and went forward he would reach home. He looked to his right and left, but there was not the faintest trace of a road anywhere. He soon explained to himself that he was probably not able to see the trunk road because of the night. The road must be there all right. He turned to his right, took a step or two, and went knee-deep in quagmire. He waded through it and went forward. Long spiked grass tickled his face and in some places he was lost in undergrowth. He turned back and reached the road.

***

Presently he realized his position. He was on an unknown distant road at a ghostly hour. Till now the hope that he was moving towards the familiar trunk road sustained him. But now even the false hope being gone, he became faint with fear. When he understood that the trunk road was an unreal distant dream, his legs refused to support him. All the same he kept tottering onwards, knowing well that it was a meaningless, aimless march. He walked like one half-stunned. The strangeness of the hour, so silent indeed that even the drop of a leaf resounded through the place, oppressed him with a sense of inhumanity. Its remoteness gave him a feeling that he was walking into a world of horrors, subhuman and supernatural.

He collapsed like an empty bag, and wept bitterly. He called to his father, mother, granny, Rajam, and Mani. His shrill, loud cry went through the night past those half-distinct black shapes looming far ahead, which might be trees or devils or gateposts of Inferno. Now he prayed to all the gods that he knew to take him out of that place. He promised them offerings: two coconuts every Saturday to the elephant-faced *Ganapathi;* a vow to roll bare-bodied in dust, beg, and take the alms to the Lord of Thirupathi. He paused as if to give the gods time to consider his offer and descend from their heights to rescue him.

Now his head was full of wild imaginings. He heard heavy footfalls behind, turned and saw a huge lump of darkness coming towards him. It was too late, it had seen him. Its immense tusks showed faintly white. It came roaring, on the way putting its long trunk around a tree and plucking it out by the roots and dashing it on the ground. He could see its small eyes, red with anger, its tusks lowered, and the trunk lifted and poised ready. He just rolled to one side and narrowly escaped. He lay panting for a while, his clothes wet with sweat. He heard stealthy footsteps and a fierce growl, and before he could turn to see what it was, heavy jaws snapped behind his ears, puffing out foul hot breath on his nape. He had the presence of mind to lower his head and lie flat, and the huge yellow-and-black tiger missed him. Now a leopard, now a lion, even a whale, now a huge crowd, a mixed crowd of wild elephants, tigers, lions, and demons, surrounded him. The demons lifted him by his ears, plucked every hair on his head, and peeled off his skin from head to foot. Now what was this, coiling round his legs, cold and slimy? He shrank in horror from a scorpion that was advancing with its sting in the air. No, this was no place for a human being. The cobra and the scorpion were within an inch of him. He shrieked, scrambled to his feet, and ran. He kept looking back, the scorpion was moving as fast as he, there was no escaping it; he held his breath and with the last ounce of strength doubled his pace—

He had touched the other wicket and returned. Two runs. He stood with the bat. The captain of the Y.M.U. bowled, and he hit a sixer. The cheers were deafening. Rajam ran round the field in joy, jumped up the wall and down thrice. The next ball was bowled. Instead of hitting it, Swaminathan flung the bat aside and received it on his head. The ball rebounded and speeded back towards the bowler—the Board High School headmaster; but Swaminathan ran after the ball, overtook it half-way, caught it, and raising his arm, let it go with terrific force towards the captain's head, which was presently hit and shattered. The M.C.C. had won, and their victory was marked by chasing the Y.M.U. out of the field, with bricks and wickets, bats and balls; and Swaminathan laughed and laughed till he collapsed with exhaustion.

***

Ranga, the cart man, was returning to his village five miles on this side of Memphis Forests, early on Saturday morning. He had left Malgudi at two in the morning, so as to be in his village by noon. He had turned the long stretch of the Memphis Forest Road, tied the bullock-rope to the cart, and lain down. The soft tinkling of the bells and the gentle steady pace of the bullock sent him to sleep at once.

Suddenly the bullock stopped with a jerk. Ranga woke up and uttered the series of oaths and driving cries that usually gave the bullock speed, and violently tugged the rope. The bullock merely tossed its head with a tremendous jingle of its bells, but did not move. Ranga, exasperated by its conduct, got down to let the animal know and feel what he thought of it. In the dim morning light, he saw a human form across the way. He shouted. "Hi! Get up, lazy lubber. A nice place you have found to sleep in! Be up and doing. Do you follow me?" When the sleeper was not awakened by this advice, Ranga went forward to throw him out of the way.

"Ah, a little fellow! Why is he sleeping here?" he said, and bending closer still, exclaimed, "Oh, *Siva,* he is dead!" The legs and arms, the exposed portions of the body, were damp with the slight early dew. He tore the boy's shirt and plunged his hand in and was greatly relieved to find the warmth of life still there. His simple mind tortured itself with the mystery of the whole situation. Here was a little boy from the town, his dress and appearance proclaimed, alone in this distant highway, lying nearly dead across the road. Who was he? Where did he come from? Why was he there? Ranga's brain throbbed with these questions. Devils were known to carry away human beings and leave them in distant places. It might be, or might not be. He gave up the attempt to solve the problem himself, feeling that he had better leave such things to learned people like the *sircar* officer who was staying in the Travellers' Bungalow three stones on this side of the forests. His (Ranga's) business would be nothing more than taking the boy to the officer. He gently lifted the boy and carried him to the cart.

He sat in his seat, took the ropes in his hand, raised a foot and kicked the bullock in the stomach, and loosened the rope with the advice to his animal that if it did not for once give up its usual dawdling ways, he would poke a red-hot pike into its side. Intelligently appreciating the spirit of this advice, the bullock shook itself and set off at a trot that it reserved for important occasions.

✳✳✳

Swaminathan stared blankly before him. He could not comprehend his situation. At first he had believed he was where he had been day after day for so many years—at home. Then gradually, as his mind cleared, he remembered several remote incidents in a confused jumble. He blinked fast. He put out his arm and fumbled about. He studied the objects before him more keenly. It was an immense struggle to keep the mind alert. He fixed his eyes on a picture on the wall—or was it a calendar?—to find out if it was the same thing that hung before his bed at home. He was understanding its details little by little when all of a sudden his mind collapsed with exhaustion, and confusion began. Was there an object there at all on the wall? He was exasperated by the pranks of the mind...He vaguely perceived a human figure in a chair nearby. The figure drew the chair nearer and said, "That is right, boy. Are you all right now?"...These words fell on ears that had not yet awakened to life. Swaminathan was puzzled to see his father there. He wanted to know why he was doing such an extraordinary thing as sitting by his side.

"Father," he cried, looking at the figure.

"You will see your father presently. Don't worry," said the figure and put to him a few questions which would occur to any man with normal curiosity. Swaminathan took such a long time to answer each question and then it was all so incoherent and irrelevant that the stranger was first amused, then irritated, and in the end gave up asking questions. Swaminathan was considerably weakened by the number of problems that beset him: Who was this man? Was he Father? If he was not, why was he there? Even if he was, why was he there? Who was he? What was he saying? Why could he not utter his words louder and clearer?

This Father-and-not-Father person then left the room. He was Mr M. P. S. Nair, the District Forest Officer, just then camping near Memphis Forests. He had been out in the forest the whole day and returned to the Travellers' Bungalow only at seven in the evening. He had hardly rolled off his puttees and taken off his heavy boots when he was told about the boy. After hours of effort with food and medicine, the boy was revived. But what was the use? He was not in a fit condition to give an account of himself. If the boy's words were to be believed, he seemed to belong to some strange unpronounceable place unknown to geographers.

Early next morning Mr Nair found the boy already up and very active. In the compound, the boy stood a few yards from a tree with a heap of stones at his feet. He stooped, picked up a stone, backed a few yards, took a few quick steps, stopped abruptly, and let the stone go at a particular point on the tree-trunk. He repeated this like clockwork with stone after stone.

"Good morning, young man," Mr Nair said. "How are you now?"

"I am grateful to you, sir, you have saved me from great trouble."

"Oh, yes...You are very busy?"

"I am taking practice, sir. We are playing a match against the Y.M.U. and Rajam is depending upon me for bowling. They call me Tate. I have not had practice at all—for—for a long time. I did a foolish thing in starting out and missing practice with the match coming off on—what day is this, sir?"

"Why do you want to know?"

"Please tell me, sir. I want to know how many days more we have for the match."

"This is Sunday."

"What? What?" Swaminathan stood petrified. Sunday! Sunday! He gazed dully at the heap of stones at his feet.

"What is the matter?"

"The match is on Sunday," Swaminathan stammered.

"What if it is? You have still a day before you. This is only Saturday."

"You said it was Sunday, sir."

"No. No. This is Saturday. See the calendar if you like."

"But you said it was Sunday."

"Probably a slip of the tongue."

"Sir, will you see that I am somehow at the field before Sunday?"

"Certainly, this very evening. But you must tell me which your place is and whose son you are."

18

THE RETURN

It was three-thirty on Sunday afternoon. The match between the M.C.C. and the Y.M.U. was still in progress. The Y.M.U. had won the toss, and were all out for eighty-six at two o'clock. The captain's was the top score, thirty-two. The M.C.C. had none to bowl him out, and he stood there like an automaton, hitting right and left, tiring out all the bowlers. He kept on for hours, and the next batsman was as formidable, though not a scorer. He exhausted the M.C.C. of the little strength that was left, and Rajam felt keenly the lack of a clever bowler.

After the interval the game started again at two-thirty, and for the hour that the M.C.C. batted the score stood at the unimpressive figure of eight with three out in quick succession. Rajam and Mani had not batted. Rajam watched the game with the blackest heart and cursed heartily everybody concerned. The match would positively close at five-thirty: just two hours more, and would the remaining eight make up at least seventy-eight and draw the match? It was a remote possibility. In his despair he felt that at least six more would follow suit without raising the score to twenty. And then he and Mani would be left. And he had a wild momentary hope that each might be able to get forty with a few judicious sixers and boundaries.

He was squatting along with his players on the ground in the shade of the compound wall.

"Raju, a minute, come here," came a voice from above. Rajam looked up and saw his father's head over the wall. "Father, is it very urgent?"

"It is. I won't detain you for more than a minute."

When he hopped over the wall and was at his father's side, he was given a letter. He glanced through it, gave it back to his father, and said casually, "So he is safe and sound. I wonder what he is doing there." He ruminated for a second and turned to go.

"I am sending this letter to Swaminathan's father. He is sure to get a car and rush to the place. I shall have to go with him. Would you like to come?"

Rajam remained silent for a minute and said emphatically, "No."

"Don't you want to see your friend and bring him back?"

"I don't care," Rajam said briefly, and joined his friends. He went back to his seat in the shade of the wall. The fourth player was promising. Rajam whispered to Mani, "I say, that boy is not bad. Six runs already! Good, good."

"If these fellows make at least fifty we can manage the rest."

Rajam nodded an assent, but an unnoticed corner of his mind began to be busy with something other than the match. His father's news had stirred in him a mixture of feelings. He felt an urgent desire to tell Mani what he had just heard. "Mani, you know Swami—" he said and stopped short because he remembered that he was not interested in Swaminathan. Mani sprang up and asked, "What about Swami? What about him? Tell me, Rajam. Has he been found?"

"I don't know."

"Oh, Rajam, Rajam, you were about to say something about him."

"Nothing. I don't care."

***

Swaminathan had a sense of supreme well-being and security. He was flattered by the number of visitors that were coming to see him. His granny and mother were hovering round him ceaselessly, and it was with a sneaking satisfaction that he saw his little brother crowing unheeded in the cradle, for once overlooked and abandoned by everybody.

Many of his father's friends came to see him and behaved more or less alike. They stared at him with amusement and said how relieved they were to have him back, and asked some stereotyped questions and went away after uttering one or two funny remarks. Father went out with one of his friends. Before going, he said, "Swami, I hope I shall not have to look for you when I come back." Swaminathan was hurt by this remark. He felt it to be cruel and inconsiderate.

After his father left he felt more free, free to lord over a mixed gathering consisting of Mother's and Granny's friends and some old men who were known to the family long before Swaminathan's father was born.

Everybody gazed at Swaminathan and uttered loud remarks to his face. Through all this crowd Swaminathan espied the cook and bestowed a smile on him. Over the babble the cook uttered some irrelevant, happy remark, which concluded with the hope that now Father, Mother and Granny might resume the practice of taking food. Swaminathan was about to shout something in reply when his attention was diverted by the statement of a widow, who, rolling her eyes and pointing heavenward, said that He alone had saved the boy, and who could have foreseen that the Forest Officer would be there to save the boy from the jaws of wild beasts? Granny said that she would have to set about fulfilling the great promises of offerings made to the Lord of the Seven Hills to whom alone she owed the safe return of the child.

Mother had meanwhile disappeared into the kitchen and now came out with a tumbler of hot coffee with plenty of sugar in it, and some steaming tiffin in a plate. Swaminathan, quickly and with great relish, disposed of both. A mixed fragrance, delicate and evocative, came from the kitchen.

Swaminathan cast his mind and felt ashamed of himself for his conduct with the Forest Officer, when that harassed gentleman was waiting for a reply from the Deputy Superintendent of Police, which took the form of a taxi drawing up before the Travellers' Bungalow, disgorging Father, Mother, Rajam's father, and an inspector of police. What a scene his mother created when she saw him! He had at first feared that Rajam's father and the inspector were going to handcuff him. What a fine man Rajam's father was! And how extraordinarily kind his own father was! So much so that, five minutes after meeting him, Swaminathan blurted out the whole story, from his evasion of drill classes to his disappearance, without concealing a single detail. What was there so funny in his narration? Everybody laughed uproariously, and Mother covered her face with the end of her *sari* and wiped her eyes at the end of every fit of laughter...This retrospect was spoiled by one memory. He had forgotten to take leave of the Forest Officer, though that gentleman opened the door of the car and stood near it. Swaminathan's conscience scorched him at the recollection of it. A gulp came to his throat at the thought of the kindly District Forest Officer, looking after the car speeding away from him, thoroughly broken-hearted by the fact that a person whose life he had saved should be so wicked as to go away without saying goodbye.

His further reflections on the subject and the quiet discussion among the visitors about the possible dangers that might have befallen Swaminathan, were all disturbed—destroyed, would be more accurate—by a tornado-like personality sweeping into their midst with the tremendous shout, "What! Oh! Swami!" The visitors were only conscious of some mingled shoutings and brisk movements and after that both Swaminathan and Mani disappeared from the hall.

As they came to a secluded spot in the backyard Mani said, "I thought you were dead or some such thing."

"I was, nearly."

"What a fool you were to get frightened of that Headmaster and run away like that! Rajam told me everything. I wanted to break your shoulders for not calling me when you had come to our school and called Rajam..."

"I had no time, Mani."

"Oh, Swami. I am so glad to see you alive. I was—I was very much troubled about you. Where were you all along?"

"I—I—I really can't say. I don't know where I was. Somewhere—" He recounted in this style his night of terrors and the subsequent events.

"Have I not always said that you were the worst coward I have ever known? You would have got safely back home if you had kept your head cool and followed the straight road. You imagined all sorts of things."

Swaminathan took this submissively and said, "But I can't believe that I was picked up by that cart man. I don't remember it at all."

Mani advised, "If he happens to come to your place during *Deepavali* or *Pongal* festival, don't behave like a niggard. He deserves a bag of gold. If he had not cared to pick you up, you might have been eaten by a tiger."

"And I have done another nasty thing," Swaminathan said, "I didn't thank and say goodbye to the Forest Officer before I came away. He was standing near the car all the time."

"If he was so near why did you seal your mouth?"

"I didn't think of it till the car had come half-way."

"You are a—a very careless fellow. You ought to have thanked him."

"Now what shall I do? Shall I write to him?"

"Do. But do you know his address?"

"My father probably does."

"What will you write?"

"Just tell him—I don't know. I shall have to ask Father about it. Some nice letter, you know. I owe him so much for bringing me back in time for the match."

"What are you saying?" Mani asked.

"Are you deaf? I was saying that I must ask Father to write a nice letter, that is all."

"Not that. I heard something about the match. What is it?"

"Yes?"

"Are you mad to think that you are in time for the match?" asked Mani. He then related to Swaminathan the day's encounter with the Y.M.U. and the depressing results, liberally explaining what Swaminathan's share was in the collapse of the M.C.C.

"Why did you have it today?" Swaminathan asked weakly.

"Why not?"

"But this is only Saturday."

"Who said that?"

"The Forest Officer said that this was only Saturday."

"You may go and tell him that he is a blockhead," Mani retorted.

Swaminathan persisted that it could not be Sunday till Mani threatened to throw him down, sit on his body, and press his entrails out. Swaminathan remained in silence, and then said, "I won't write him that letter. He has deceived me."

"Who?"

"The Forest Officer...And what does Rajam say about me?"

"Rajam says a lot, which I don't wish to repeat. But I will tell you one thing. Never appear before him. He will never speak to you. He may even shoot you on sight."

"What have I done?" asked Swaminathan.

"You have ruined the M.C.C. You need not have promised us, if you had wanted to funk. At least you could have told us you were going away. Why did you hide it from Rajam when you saw him at our school? That is what Rajam wants to know."

Swaminathan quietly wept, and begged Mani to pacify Rajam and convey to him Swaminathan's love and explanations. Mani refused to interfere. "You don't know Rajam. He is a gem. But it is difficult to get on with him."

With a forced optimism in his tone Swaminathan said, "He will be all right when he sees me. I shall see him tomorrow morning."

Mani wanted to change the topic, and asked: "Are you going back to school?"

"Yes, next week. My father has already seen the headmaster, and it seems things will be all right in the school. He seems to have known everything about the Board School business."

"Yes, I and Rajam told him everything."

"After all, I shall have to go back to the Board High School. Father says I can't change my school now."

19

PARTING PRESENT

On Tuesday morning, ten days later, Swaminathan rose from bed with a great effort of will at five o'clock. There was still half an hour for the train to arrive at the Malgudi Station and leave it four minutes later, carrying away Rajam for ever.

Swaminathan had not known that this was to happen till Mani came and told him, on the previous night at about ten, that Rajam's father was transferred to Trichinopoly and the whole family would be leaving Malgudi on the following morning. Mani said that he had known it for about a week, but Rajam had strictly forbidden him to say anything about it to Swaminathan. But at the last moment Mani could not contain himself and had violated Rajam's ban.

A great sense of desolation seized Swaminathan at once. The world seemed to have become blank all of a sudden. The thought of Lawley Extension without Rajam appalled him with its emptiness. He swore that he would never go there again. He raved at Mani. And Mani bore it patiently. Swaminathan could not think of a world without Rajam. What was he to do in the evenings? How was he to spend the holiday afternoons? Whom was he to think of as his friend? At the same time he was filled with a sense of guilt: he had not gone and seen Rajam even once after his return. Fear, shame, a feeling of uncertainty, had made him postpone his visit to Rajam day after day. Twice he had gone up to the gate of Rajam's house but had turned back, his courage and determination giving way at the last moment. He was in this state, hoping to see Rajam every tomorrow, when Mani came to him with the shattering news. Swaminathan wanted to rush up to Rajam's house that very second and claim him once again. But—but—he felt awkward and shirked. Tomorrow morning at the station. The train was leaving at six. He would go to the station at five.

"Mani, will you call me at five tomorrow morning?"

"No. I am going to sleep in Rajam's house, and go with him to the station."

For a moment Swaminathan was filled with the darkest jealousy. Mani to sleep in Rajam's house, keep him company till the last moment, talk and laugh till midnight, and he to be excluded! He wanted to cling to Mani desperately and stop his going.

When Mani left, Swaminathan went in, opened his dealwood box, and stood gazing into it. He wanted to pick out something that could be presented to Rajam on the following morning. The contents of the box were a confused heap of odds and ends of all metals and materials. Here a cardboard box that had once touched Swaminathan's fancy, and there a toy watch, a catalogue, some picture-books, nuts and bolts, disused insignificant parts of defunct machinery, and so on to the brim. He rummaged in it for half an hour, but there seemed to be nothing worth taking to Rajam. The only decent object in it was a green engine given to him over a year ago by Rajam. The sight of it, now dented and chipped in a couple of places and lying between an empty thread-reel and a broken porcelain vase, stirred in him vivid memories. He became maudlin...He wondered if he would have to return that engine to Rajam now that they were no longer friends. He picked it up to take it with him to the station and return it to Rajam. On second thoughts he put it back, partly because he loved the engine very much, partly because he told himself that it might be an insult to reject a present after such a long time...Rajam was a good reader, and Swaminathan decided to give him a book. He could not obviously give him any of the textbooks. He took out the only book that he respected (as the fact of his separating it from the textbooks on his desk and giving it a place in the dealwood box showed). It was a neat tiny volume of Andersen's *Fairy Tales* that his father had bought in Madras years ago for him. He could never get through the book to his satisfaction. There were too many unknown, unpronounceable

English words in it. He would give this book to Rajam. He went to his desk and wrote on the fly-leaf 'To my dearest friend Rajam.'

✳✳✳

Malgudi Station was half dark when Swaminathan reached it with the tiny volume of Andersen's *Fairy Tales* in his hand. The station-master was just out of bed and was working at the table with a kerosene light, not minding in the least the telegraph keys that were tapping away endless messages to the dawn.

A car drew up outside. Swaminathan saw Rajam, his father, mother, someone he did not know, and Mani, getting down. Swaminathan shrank at the sight of Rajam. All his determination oozed out as he saw the captain approach the platform, dressed like a 'European boy'. His very dress and tidiness made Swaminathan feel inferior and small. He shrank back and tried to make himself inconspicuous.

Almost immediately, the platform began to fill with police officers and policemen. Rajam was unapproachable. He was standing with his father in the middle of a cluster of people in uniform. All that Swaminathan could see of Rajam was his left leg, through a gap between two policemen. Even that was obstructed when the policemen drew closer. Swaminathan went round, in search of further gaps.

The train was sighted. There was at once a great bustle. The train hissed and boomed into the platform. The hustle and activity increased. Rajam and his party moved to the edge of the platform. Things were dragged and pushed into a Second Class compartment with desperate haste by a dozen policemen. Rajam's mother got in. Rajam and his father were standing outside the compartment. The police officers now barricaded them completely, bidding them farewell and garlanding them. There was a momentary glimpse of Rajam with a huge rose garland round his neck.

Swaminathan looked for and found Mani. "Mani, Rajam is going away."

"Yes, Swami, he is going away."

"Mani, will Rajam speak to me?"

"Oh, yes. Why not?" asked Mani.

Now Rajam and his father had got into the compartment. The door was closed and the door-handle turned.

"Mani, this book must be given to Rajam," Swaminathan said. Mani saw that there was no time to lose. The bell rang. They desperately pushed their way through the crowd and stood under a window. Swaminathan could hardly see anything above. His head hardly came up to the door-handle. The crowd pressed from behind. Mani shouted into the compartment: "Here is Swami to bid you goodbye." Swaminathan stood on his toes. A head leaned over the window and said: "Goodbye, my Mani. Don't forget me. Write to me."

"Goodbye, friend … Here is Swami," Mani said.

Rajam craned his neck. Swaminathan's upturned eyes met his. At the sight of the familiar face

Swaminathan lost control of himself and cried: "Oh, Rajam, Rajam, you are going away, away. When will you come back?"

Rajam kept looking at him without a word and then (as it seemed to Swaminathan) opened his mouth to say something, when everything was disturbed by the guard's blast and the hoarse whistle of the engine. There was a slight rattling of chains, a tremendous hissing, and the train began to move. Rajam's face, with the words still unuttered on his lips, receded.

Swaminathan became desperate and blurted: "Oh, Mani! This book must be given to him," and pressed the book into Mani's hand.

Mani ran along the platform with the train and shouted over the noise of the train: "Goodbye, Rajam. Swami gives you this book." Rajam held out his hand for the book, and took it, and waved a farewell. Swaminathan waved back frantically.

Swaminathan and Mani stood as if glued where they were, and watched the train. The small red lamp of the last van could be seen for a long time, it diminished in size every minute, and disappeared around a bend. All the jarring, rattling, clanking, spurting, and hissing of the moving train softened in the distance into something that was half a sob and half a sigh. Swaminathan said: "Mani, I am glad he has taken the book. Mani, he waved to me. He was about to say something when the train started. Mani, he did wave to me and to me alone. Don't deny it."

"Yes, yes," Mani agreed.

Swaminathan broke down and sobbed.

Mani said: "Don't be foolish, Swami."

"Does he ever think of me now?" Swaminathan asked hysterically.

"Oh, yes," said Mani. He paused and added: "Don't worry. If he has not talked to you, he will write to you."

"What do you mean?"

"He told me so," Mani said.

"But he does not know my address."

"He asked me, and I have given it," said Mani.

"No. No. It is a lie. Come on, tell me, what is my address?"

"It is—it is—never mind what...I have given it to Rajam."

Swaminathan looked up and gazed on Mani's face to find out whether Mani was joking or was in earnest. But for once Mani's face had become inscrutable.